CICADA

Look for other Western & Adventure novels by
Eric H. Heisner

Along to Presidio

West to Bravo

Seven Fingers a' Brazos

T. H. Elkman

Short Western Tales: Friend of the Devil

Wings of the Pirate

Africa Tusk

Conch Republic, Island Stepping with Hemingway

Follow book releases and film productions at:
www.leandogproductions.com

CICADA

Eric H. Heisner

Illustrations by Adeline Emmalei

Visit our website at
www.leandogproductions.com

Illustrations by: Adeline Emmalei

Dustcover jacket design: Dreamscape Cover Designs

Paperback ISBN: 978-1-7353257-1-2

Printed in the United States of America

Inspiration

The blessings of growing up in a small,
rural, farming community

Special Thanks

Tim Haughian, Adeline Heisner
& Amber Word Heisner

Note from Author

Small towns have a certain life-force of their own. It is said that if two people know something, then twenty know it. I grew up in a small Midwestern town with a population of just a few thousand people. There were no chain restaurants, the first stop & go light was put in while I was in High School, and the historic downtown still has a building from when the stagecoach line passed through.

During my first two years of college, I worked for the city's public works department. Some of my tasks included filling potholes, chipping brush in the summer and plowing snow in the winter, but most of the time the hours were filled with just trying to keep busy. One of my best friends worked along with me, and we were once tasked with repainting the crosswalks and parking lines on the main street. This had to happen during the dead of night, and our breaks were spent hanging out at the local police station. Long overnight work shifts get the mind to racing, and you never know what sort of stories the mind will dredge up.

Now, I'm not saying I know some of the characters in this fictional tale, but I might…

Eric H. Heisner

June 20, 2020

Chapter 1

After the temperatures of winter have passed, and before the steaminess of summertime arrives, a warming rain has brought spring to the isolated farming town of Burlingview. As the sun nears the horizon, the mercury vapor bulbs of the lamps along the main avenue begin to pop on and illuminate. Like the orchestra sound check before a concert, the clicking sound of cicadas rises to a deafening chatter that fills the air of the coming night.

A Studebaker farm truck, about nineteen-forty vintage, rolls down the main street of town and parks in front of the local drinking establishment. Extending out over the sidewalk, a neon sign flashes and brightly glows above the bar's entrance door. It reads: *Hall's Tap*. A random, middle-aged man, outfitted in the rural work uniform of denim jeans, cowboy boots and a faded, cotton, snap-front shirt, steps out of the old truck and ambles inside the public drinking house. The barroom door swings closed again, blocking the sounds of music from inside. The evening air of the town drones with the buzzing of streetlights and the chatter of insects.

~*~

Fresh-faced, early in his twenties and wearing a college sports club shirt with the team logo ironed across the front, John Bratcher walks up to the entry of the only pub in town. A florescent beer sign in the window glows red on his features while the lit sign over the door casts shadows under his eyes. He hesitates to enter and instead walks down the block of sidewalk to the corner of the building. John strolls down the walkway between buildings and examines a riding lawn-tractor, parked mid-alleyway, with two new cans of unopened beer tucked under the seat springs. He lets out a snort and smiles to himself, as he tucks his t-shirt into his waistband and walks back to the front of the building. The muted sounds of music playing and bar patrons talking becomes louder and more distinct, as John pulls open the entry door and steps inside the smoky barroom.

It takes a moment for John's eyes to adjust from the bright neon outside to the dimly-lit interior of the local watering hole. He works his way to the long bar, recognizing familiar faces as he scans the crowded room. Stopping next to an old man hunched on a red-vinyl barstool, he reaches over to pat him along the shoulders. "What happened, Sticky? I saw your old ride parked back in the alley. You lose your driver's license again?"

The drunken man on the bar stool, hunkered over a glass of beer, seems to startle slightly at the affectionate touch. He pivots on his high-seated stool and grimaces aside at John. All of a sudden, he breaks

Cicada

into a friendly, half-toothed grin. "Shit yeah. Damn pigs are always trying to bring us down." As John nods his enthusiastic agreement with mock seriousness, Sticky gives a throaty, chuckling laugh and lifts a single, stubby key on a John Deere patterned keychain fob. "Don't need a damned license to drive this bad-boy though." Sticky giggles amiably and proclaims, "You should see that sucker go when I push it to the bunny rabbit!"

"Hey Sticky, you'd be better to keep it on turtle."

Joining the old man in amused laughter, John leans back against the rail of the bar and looks out over the crowd. He spots one of his friends, Frank, from his high school days, standing before the jukebox with a palm-full of quarters. Nearby, at a big, round table, he sees two other schoolmates, Tom and Chris, having their nightly round of drinks.

Pocketing his coins after finishing his selection of music, Frank notices John at the bar and waves him over. "Hey John, come over here." After acknowledging the wave, John leans on the bar to catch the attention of the bartender. "Sammy, I'll take one of whatever is tonight's *Low-priced Special*."

The oversized bartender in the extra-large uniform, sport-jersey and baseball cap nods and shuffles over while tugging his shirt from sticking between his chest and belly. "Sure, Johnny. Looks like its Blue Ribbon tonight."

"That'll be fine, thanks."

Behind the bartender, on the wall, a 1965 calendar reads: *If you weren't born before 1944, you can't drink it here.* Sammy, the bartender, pulls a canned beer from a trough of crushed ice and pops the top on the can. He sets it on a coaster for John and leans heavily on the bar slab with both hands. "That'll be fifty cents. You been keeping up and playing much baseball at that city college of yours?"

John lays out a dollar and takes a sip from the beer. "Naw, haven't had any time. The engineering program is pretty tough."

The hefty bartender swipes the single dollar bill off the bar top and slaps down two quarters for change in its place, "If you're up for it, we're gonna get some of the boys together to play a ballgame this weekend out at Lust's Field..."

John gives an accommodating smile to the bartender and looks over at the table with his old, high-school friends. He slides the coins from the bar and puts them in his pocket. "Sounds fun. I'll mostly be around my folk's hardware store." Giving the older man on the stool another pat on the shoulder, John walks over to the large table with Frank, Tom and Chris. A warm greeting is exchanged by all, as they settle into another night of their usual drinking.

Chapter 2

An almost ridiculous amount of beer bottles and aluminum cans have accumulated at the center of the big round table. Sammy shuffles around from behind the bar and shakes his head, laughing as he sets down another round of drinks. "Want me to take some of these away, guys?"

Chris pipes up, "Hell no! How'll we know what we've all accomplished tonight if you clean the slate?"

Sammy takes a five dollar bill from Frank and shuffles off to his position behind the bar. "You guys are gonna be useless at the ballgame tomorrow."

Tom finishes his beer and slides the empty can to the center of the table before stacking it on the others. "Who says we won't be able to play with a bit of a hangover?"

Chris belches, pretends to chew it and grins proudly. "Ya won't ever get a hangover if you never stop drinking." The two laugh, looking to the fresh cans and single bottle.

John grabs one of the beer cans and takes a swig, as Tom and Chris fight over the lone, amber bottle of Coors. Chris, defeated in the friendly scuffle, peers over at John. "How long is it again you plan to stay in town, Johnny-boy?"

Tom has a drink then swats Chris across the shoulder and groans, "Dammit Chris, he told you ten times already!"

John takes another sip from his drink and laughs. "The week is all, and then I have to get back to school."

Taking the remaining beverage, Frank spins his baseball cap around backwards on his head and sits upright. Surprisingly, he finishes off the full can of beer in one long, gulping swallow, and then stands with his arms spread wide. "Who needs another one?" He wags his finger around the table, counting, and smiles at John, who looks to the freshly opened can before him.

Frank stifles a belch and giggles, amused at them all. "Fuck man, you're milking those like a damn dairy farmer." Moving around the table, Frank pats John on the shoulder, gives him a friendly shake and stumbles off toward the bar. Seated across from John, Chris finishes his beer, crunches up the empty can and snickers, "I thought everyone in college was a big drinker. Drink up, Johnny-boy!"

Giving into peer pressure, John lifts his can of beer to gulp down most of it, then sets it aside, and takes a breath. "There you go. I can still drink to keep up with you bums."

Cicada

Finishing his can of beer, Tom chimes, "Come on! One more!"

The objects in the room start to slant in a blur and the music echoes loudly in his head as John wavers in his chair seat in a display of apparent drunkenness. He shakes off the feeling and looks to his school friends across the messy table. "I have to take it a bit easy. I borrowed my roommate's car for the week, and I can't afford to crack it up."

Frank returns to the table with four more beers gathered between his hands and places one in front of John. "Drink up to old times! We played some good ball in school." They all clank their full drinks together and chug the contents. Everyone practically finishes the full measure except John. Tom spins his empty can on the table and slurs, "Drink up man... I'll drive you home."

Leaning his chair back, on two legs, John fiddles with the beer can, its last remains swishing around inside. "Do you guys know if Mike is home from the Academy this weekend?"

Chris piles his empty can in the middle of the big table and replies, "Probably... He comes back on the weekends to visit his mom."

Tom holds the edge of the table, shaking it, and utters. "Things haven't changed too much for Mike. He doesn't really hang with us here and will always be a momma's boy."

Chris laughs and comments, "Hell, I'm surprised he even went off to the big city for police academy."

Tom nods. "Did you know that he breast fed until he was twelve?"

Eric H. Heisner

Smiling at them, Frank's eyes light up with excitement. "With his mom, I don't blame him. That's why he's so smart." He looks at John with a chuckle. "Hey John, what about you? You're pretty smart too."

Everyone at the table tilts their heads back laughing at the juvenile suggestion and then continues drinking. There is a momentary lull in the conversation until Frank breaks it. "You know that his mom gave in and married Russling?" John practically chokes on his gulp of beer. "Deputy Russling, the asshole?" Frank nods affirmatively. "Yep. The same one who sent Robbie to juvie. Now he's the Sherriff."

Pushing his chair back to get another round of beers, Chris leans over the table and whispers, a bit too loudly, "Mike's mom is still a hottie. Russling had his eyes on her since Mike's dad skipped town, and probably even before."

John takes a swig of beer and rolls his eyes in his head. "Shit, I knew that, but damn, she actually married him, huh?" He drinks again and stares away in disbelief at the news.

They watch Chris grab four more beers for them at the bar and walk back. Tom looks to John who seems in a daze. "You haven't talked to Mike in a while?"

John breaks from his contemplating stare. "Guess not. What does he think about it?"

Chris sets the next round of beers on the table and passes them around. "He hates the guy, but you know he'd never say shit to his mom though."

8

Cicada

John takes up one of the new beers and knocks back another swig. "Think I'll head on over to see if he's around."

Frank finishes his beer and takes another from Chris. "Good time to do it. Ol' Russling is out of town for the night." He takes a drink and continues. "He's in the city for a convention or something."

Confounded, Tom looks across the table at Frank. "Where'd you hear that?"

Frank grins at Tom and replies, "I've got connections." He tips back his beer again and laughs. "Dodds, the deputy, plays softball with me on Wednesdays." Frank sets his beer down and shrugs. "Since Russling is out of town, he said I could ride along with him tonight if I wanted."

Appearing a bit jealous, Tom puts on a pouting face. "What are you going to do, make out in the back of the car?"

Tom laughs at his own joke, as Frank lets out a huge, chest-thundering belch and replies, "We're gonna listen to the police scanner for reports of you driving home or hope for a high-speed chase through the middle of town." Frank smirks at Tom then turns to John. "You should come along with us. Didn't Dodds coach you one year in track?"

John shrugs a shoulder as he thinks back to those days. "Gosh, haven't seen him since high school."

Tom snubs out his cigarette and flicks it at Frank. "Hey shithead, why the fuck didn't you invite me?"

Frank fires back snidely, "You wouldn't know how to ride in a squad car without handcuffs on."

Finishing off his beer, John stands at the table to leave. "I'm gonna head over to Mike's and see what he's up to." Chris looks over at the bartender and then back toward John. "You playing ball this weekend?"

"I should be around to play. See you guys later."

Frank lifts his beer in a salute. "See ya."

John steadies himself on the backrest of the bar chair and comically takes a long, deep, inhale then rolls his eyes. Unexpectedly, a pair of female hands comes from behind and embraces him around the middle. John visibly startles and everyone laughs uproariously. He turns to come face to face with a sweet, nice-looking girl about his age, Mary Rogers. "Damn, Mary! You scared the shit out of me."

Mary has a small town way about her as she smiles. "Sorry John... I didn't know you were so jumpy. I just wanted to get your attention."

John gathers himself together and frowns. "What are you up to? I was going to try and call you later."

She looks at him acutely, as if only half-believing what he is saying. "I heard you were in town, so I figured you'd come down here first to see these clowns."

The boys around the table giggle and put on silly faces. John waves them off and asks Mary, "You have detectives out on me already? I just got back into town a few hours ago."

Mary's cheeks flush red, embarrassed, and she replies, "It's a small town, John. You can't keep secrets around here."

Frank slaps his palm on the table and blurts out, "Not from Mary at least!"

Cicada

John laughs uneasily and steps backward. "Yeah, well, I have to go. See you all later."

He gives a wave to his friends at the table and moves around Mary toward the exit. Mary follows behind John and reaches out to catch him just as he opens the front door. "John… Wait."

He stops, hesitates, and turns uncomfortably. "Yeah?"

Her face begins to show hurt emotions, but she controls herself as she speaks low, "I thought we could talk a minute."

John stands at the open door to the bar. "Not now. Mary, I just got back."

The pleading sentiment shows in her eyes and face. "How is tomorrow for you then?"

Unable to meet her gaze, John looks first at his shoes and then outside. "Tomorrow is fine."

Mary puts on a smile and takes a step toward John as he turns to leave. She whispers quietly to him. "I love you." He nods as he slips out the door and is gone, into the night.

Chapter 3

17 years later ...

The small town of Burlingview has seen economic change over the years but hasn't altered noticeably in appearance. Along the quiet main street, several vacant storefronts present the familiar display of rural decline. A young, police deputy walks up to a single-story, brick building just around the corner from the courthouse, looks at his watch and goes inside. The signage over the front door, once illuminated but not lit up in a long time, simply reads: *Police Station*.

The deputy pours a cup of coffee from the tall, silver canister on the table near the door and glances at the thin, morning paper. After scanning the editor's column on the second page, he folds the paper up and tucks it under his arm. He stirs some cream and sugar into the black coffee, and then he looks to the receptionist steadily typing at the front desk.

Eric H. Heisner

Walking through the untidy, open-concept office space, the receptionist merely glances up as she continues her typing. He nods to her while stepping behind a neat and extremely uncluttered workspace. The newly-printed nameplate on the desk reads: *Deputy Michael Connolly*.

Pressed and tucked-in proper in his police uniform, Mike Connolly presents himself in the image of law enforcement personnel from popular TV culture of his time; not as awkward as Barney Fife, but still far from the cool of Starsky & Hutch. He stands behind his spotlessly clean desk, places the folded newspaper in the empty corner tray and tosses his keys on top. Mike sets his coffee cup down on a coaster and looks around the desktop, becoming agitated. "Mary? Have you seen those file reports on those kids doing public service? I thought I left them right here."

Seated at the desk nearest the front of the police station, Mary Rogers stops her typing to offer an apologetic frown. She hasn't changed much in appearance over the last dozen and a half years since she was a love-struck kid, still in school. "The sheriff grabbed the files and said he'd take care of them. Guess he had something special in mind."

Mike pulls his desk chair back and takes a seat. Perturbed, he shakes his head. "Damn it! He will have them doing prison labor on his ranch as punishment for graffiti." Mary shrugs, waits a moment, then turns back to her typing.

Mike swivels his desk chair and casts a glance at all the wall decorations of the small-town police station.

Cicada

He looks to several public service award certificates and special town-event photos displayed in inexpensive, black plastic frames. His eyes wander from the line of stacked file cabinets to the single doorway and windows along the rear wall. He stares at the frosted glass windowpanes and split-panel, wood door leading to the sheriff's private office.

Turning his chair to glance toward the front entryway, Mike calls out loudly over the chattering sounds of typing. "Anything on the schedule for today?"

Not looking up from the soft-humming electronic typewriter, Mary continues to click away as she replies, "Sorry, City-Boy. Nothing on the town event calendar today." Her typing fingers halt and linger mid-keystroke, and she half-turns to glance over her shoulder at the town deputy. "Mister Thompson called about his neighbor's dog, though. Said he was going to shoot it next time it got into his trash."

Mike tilts backward in his creaking chair while Mary returns to her typing. He takes a deep, lingering breath, stares at the yellow-tinged, dirty ceiling tiles above and rocks gently. Finally, he pushes his chair back, stands up and grabs his ring of keys from the corner paper tray on the desk. "I'm going to run some errands." He pushes in his chair and asks Mary, "You need anything while I'm out?"

She leans over and slides a yellow pad of legal paper from the jumbled mess on her desk. "How far you going and how many days do you have?"

Mike walks over and hoists his hip to the edge of her paper-piled desk and glimpses the length of her

Eric H. Heisner

shopping list. "I was just planning on strolling to the café, but according to my not-so-busy schedule, I seem to have all week." He fiddles with a pen on her desk and looks out the glass doors of the police station. "The way it's been, probably next week too."

Mary smiles and puts her list on top of the paper stack. "It's the same town you grew up in. This is as busy as it gets." The electronic typewriter continues to hum low and Mary swipes the finished page from the roller bar. "You'll get used to it after you get that city-life out of your blood, Big-Shot."

Mike stands and peers over at her tablet of paper. "Anything you absolutely need on there?"

She pushes back her chair and pulls two loose keys from her top drawer. "Could you swing by the hardware store and make copies of these?"

Mike takes the pair of keys and folds them into his palm. "Sure thing, Mary. What sorts of town secrets do you have locked up with these?" He tucks them inside the breast pocket on his uniform shirt and, jiggling his own keys in hand, he exits the police station.

Chapter 4

A police squad car drives down the half mile stretch of town, turns around at a closed-down service station at the end of the strip and stops by the gas pumps. Sitting behind the wheel, Mike gazes through the windshield at the nearly empty town. He chews his lip, glances both ways, despite the absence of any traffic, and drives the car back into the street.

The squad car cruises around the town square and swings into a parking spot in front of *Bratcher's Hardware & Supply*. Mike puts the squad car in park and leans forward, low over the steering wheel, to gaze reminiscently at the two-story brick building before him. Breaking himself from his wandering thoughts of growing up, Mike steps out of the car and approaches the main entrance.

A chiming bell attached to the top of the entry door rings when Mike steps inside. He walks up to the unattended front counter, looks around a minute, then turns his attention to the items along the register displays. A voice from behind startles him as an older woman steps from the nearest aisle. "Good morning, Mike. Good to see you?"

The uniformed town deputy spins on his heel to greet Mrs. Bratcher, the mother of his old childhood friend, John. She smiles kindly at him and he returns the friendly greeting. "Good morning. How have you and Mister Bratcher been?"

In her sixties, slight and small-framed, Mrs. Bratcher moves behind the counter and shuffles items by the register. "Oh, things are fine. Anything I can help you with today?" She straightens a display and swipes dust from the counter. "Mister Bratcher hasn't come in yet this morning."

Mike reaches into his shirt pocket and pulls out the pair of keys to be duplicated. He places them on the counter with a snapping sound and slides them over to Mrs. Bratcher. "Could I please get a copy of these?"

Grinning, the older woman sweeps the keys from the counter and into her hand. "Sure, I'll do them now."

Mike smiles appreciatively and steps away to wander one of the aisles. "Thanks."

Walking toward the back of the store, Mike's ears perk at the sound of voices coming from the supply room. Surprised, he glances toward the front counter and observes Mrs. Bratcher still there, setting up the key-making machine. He moves closer to the supply room door and the loud grind of keys being made suddenly fills the air. Faintly, he can still hear the low tone of conversation as he peers through the small round window on the closed door.

Mike feels sharp pangs of dismay wash over his body, as he looks across the hardware supply room and catches a glimpse of two people talking at the rear loading dock doors. Through the clutter of items on the stocked shelves and the blinding daylight streaming in behind, he thinks he sees his childhood friend, John Bratcher, talking with his father. Fighting the weakness in his knees, Mike tries to open the supply room door only to find it locked.

Cranking the handle repeatedly, Mike tries to yell but only lets out a faint whimper, "John...?"

The conversing twosome at the loading dock doors glance over at him and then quickly duck away from view. Mike lets go of the supply room handle and stumbles into the shelving unit behind him. He rushes through the store toward the front counter as the metal-grinding sound of the key-making machine continues to echo through the stocked aisles. At the end of the aisle, Mike trips over a display of cleaners and staggers back to keep them all from tumbling over.

The loud, metal-cutting sound of the key-copy machine stops abruptly, and Mrs. Bratcher rushes around the counter to come to Mike's aid. "Are you okay, Mike? What is wrong?" He tries to sidestep around her but can't seem to make it clear, as his thoughts are muddled with the shock of seeing his old friend, still alive. She grips his shoulder and her voice comes at him muted and seemingly far away, "Mike, what's wrong?"

Eric H. Heisner

Finally, tearing himself away from her helping grasp, Mike stumbles to the entrance door and pushes it only to be met with resistance. He looks dejectedly back at Mrs. Bratcher, as if she had purposefully locked him inside. Mike pushes against the window glass again before looking down at the *pull* label over the handle.

Chapter 5

The door to the hardware store swings inward, and Mike bursts out to the sidewalk. After he quickly looks both ways, he dashes across the building front and around the corner. Crashing through the hedge row near the loading dock, he sees the doors padlocked closed.

An older man in his sixties steps out of his pickup truck and walks toward Mike at the rear corner of the building. "Good morning Michael. Is there something the matter?"

Mike looks to the father of his childhood friend and gasps, "Mister Bratcher?" He stares suspiciously at the older man, then to the loading dock doors, while he pants for air, not believing his own eyes.

Mr. Bratcher steps closer and narrows an eye at Mike. "Are you okay, Mike? You were a little hard on those bushes."

Mike continues to consider the locked loading dock doors and murmurs softly, "Where is he?"

Completely taken aback, Mr. Bratcher tilts his head and looks to Mike. "Who?"

Mike turns to the older gentleman and searches his features for any hint of an answer. "John..."

Appearing upset, Mr. Bratcher seems confused and puts his hand on Mike's shoulder to help settle him down. "Are you feeling okay, Michael?"

The deputy twists away from the comforting hold of his friend's father and looks to the unoccupied pickup truck. "I saw him back here with you."

Mr. Bratcher stares with a blank expression on his face. "Who are you talking about?

A subtle tone of irritation grips Mike's voice, as he senses a deception being put upon him. "John! Where is he?" Mike trots over to the side alley, gazes down the empty corridor and then back to the rear entry of the building again. He paces around the truck to inspect it for any signs of hiding.

Mr. Bratcher stands his ground behind the hardware store and appears hurt at the mention of his son's name. "Michael, he's been gone a few years now."

Mike completes his circuit of the truck perimeter and stares unforgivingly into the older man's eyes. "Where is he?"

The deputy's intense gaze scrutinizes John's father, until Mrs. Bratcher comes around the line of bushes and interrupts. "Mike, what happened to you? What's wrong?"

Mr. Bratcher goes to his wife and takes her arm. "It's okay now, Dear. You go back inside and I'll be there in a moment."

Cicada

Confused, she looks at her husband and replies in a whisper, "What's going on?"

He lowers his voice to match hers and tells his wife, "Michael is having a rough day. He thought he saw our son John."

The mention of her absent son brings a glistening of tears to her eyes, and she murmurs, "Oh, Mike…"

Mr. Bratcher pats her hand gently and ushers her back around the row of shrubs toward the street entrance in front. "It's okay now… Go back inside, and you mind the store." Mrs. Bratcher reluctantly turns to shuffle alongside the building and around the corner.

Mr. Bratcher watches her and then looks back to Mike. "She still gets very distraught at the thought of our lost son. Are you going to be okay, Michael?"

Feeling terrible, following the sight of the distressed older woman, Mike nods and gazes around self-consciously. "Yeah, I'm sorry about this."

Mr. Bratcher takes a breath and hunches his shoulders. "It's okay… We all loved him. Sometimes I think I see him too, as if he was never missing." The older man pats his pockets for something that isn't there. "I need to go and help Mrs. Bratcher. Are you going to be alright?"

Mike nods his head and looks to the empty truck cab. "Yes, I'm going to hang out here and pull myself together." Mr. Bratcher nods with understanding and begins to walk around the bushes to the alley leading to the front of the store. Mike watches, clears his throat and calls after him, "Mister Bratcher! Hold on a moment…?"

The old gentleman stops and turns to face him. "Yes, Michael?"

The deputy removes his gaze from his friend's father and stares suspiciously at the pair of locked doors. "Don't you usually go in the back entrance?"

Mr. Bratcher stands quietly and pats his pockets again. He puts on a smile and follows Mike's gaze to the loading dock doorway, where a set of keys dangle from the lock. Without missing a beat, the hardware man walks over and unlocks the pair of doors. "Yes... Thank you. I thought I had left my keys at home." He pulls the set of keys from the door lock and holds them in his hand, as he glimpses over at Mike. "I guess not."

Mike watches his friend's father enter the rear storeroom and quickly disappear inside. He glances back to the empty pickup truck and murmurs aloud to himself, "Guess not..."

Chapter 6

Inside the Burlingview police station, Mike sits at his desk and stares at the shuttered window blinds across the room. Finally, he lowers his gaze, opens a desk drawer and pulls out a floppy-paper book. He flips open the phone directory and scans through several pages before placing his finger on the number he seeks. Mike dials the numbers on the rotary desk phone and holds the handheld receiver up alongside his ear. The dial tone is replaced by the droning pulse of a busy signal.

Mike reaches out and taps the hang-up trigger on the receiver base and looks to the phone book again. This time he puts his index finger to a small square advertisement for *Frank's Garage and Towing Service*. His finger spins around the rotary dial again, until the tone is switched to a ringing chime. A voice on the other end of the line answers, and Mike replies, "Hello, Frank?" There is a drawn-out pause on the telephone line. "It's Mike Connolly. I need to talk to you about something."

The distant voice on the end of the line seems reticent in reply. "No, nothing's wrong. Do you think you could come down to the station sometime today?" Mike props the phone receiver against his shoulder, looks out the window at nothing in particular and then replies, "Okay. See you about lunchtime."

The line disconnects and Mike remains sitting in the chair, listening to the pulsing sound of the ended phone call. He hangs up the receiver, spins away from his desk and goes to the file cabinets near the sheriff's office door. Scanning his eyes along the drawer labels, he pulls open the first one, labeled "A - D".

~*~

The rattle of the metal rail slide on the file drawer slams closed with a bang, and Mike stands before the cabinets. Exasperated, he thumbs through two, small file folders and then tosses them to the floor. A frustrated anger boils just beneath the surface, as he calls out to the receptionist, "Mary, could you come over here?"

Peeking around from the reception area, Mary lifts a curious eyebrow toward John. "Who are you trying to find?"

Mike turns to her, surprised at her informed inquiry. "Was I looking for someone?"

Her eyes open wide with dismay. "I may not have the big-city detective training you have, but I can see when something is bothering you." She glances down at the files on the floor. "You've obviously been looking for something, huffing and puffing, trying to slam every one of the drawers."

Cicada

The reality of this sinks in, and Mike tries to calm himself down somewhat. "Sorry, I just had a bad morning." She nods her head and waits patiently for further questions. Mike gathers the two files from the floor and puts them at the center of his empty desktop. He sits on the edge and crosses his arms in thought.

Mary waits a moment before interrupting his musing. "Were you going to ask me something?"

Mike turns to her with a faraway look on his face while pensively chewing on his lip. "I've looked all through these file cabinets and haven't found a single complete file on the John Bratcher case. There are only a few odds and ends." He watches her surprisingly stunned reaction with curiosity. "What is it filed under?"

She glances toward the front entrance of the police station and back at Mike before answering quietly, "Why are you looking for that one?"

The deputy looks behind at the two meager files on his desk and back to the office secretary. "I just want to check something out."

Again, Mary discreetly looks around the room before letting her eyes settle on the closed door of the sheriff's office. Mike follows her gaze as she replies, "Sheriff Russling keeps that one in his personal files."

"What... Why?"

Mary shrugs innocently. "You asked me where it's at. He keeps some files in his office cabinet. I don't know why." Mike stands up from leaning on the desk and stares toward the dark, glass windows of the sheriff's office. He puts on a grateful smile, for her sake, and notices her waiting for any other inquiries from him.

Eric H. Heisner

"Alright, thanks. That's all for now." She stares back at him and remains, watching him.

"Mary, you can go back to whatever you were doing." Standing uncomfortably under his gaze, she shrugs and finally turns away, returning to her desk. Mike stands under the ceiling's buzzing florescent bulbs, staring at the closed door to the sheriff's office.

Chapter 7

The hanging blinds clank against the glass paneled door of the sheriff's private office when it swings inward to open. Inside the darkened room, slashes of sunlight come through the partly closed shutters. Mike stands at the threshold, peering into the diffusely-lit interior of the office. "Hello...?" He instinctively looks over his shoulder and proceeds inside.

His attention goes directly to the group of file cabinets under the long row of windows. Mike goes first to the top drawer, attempting to pull it open, only to find it locked. Frustrated, he steps around the big desk at the end of the room and pulls open the center drawer, looking for a key.

The contents of the drawer clink together as Mike pokes through the random bits of papers and personal items. Suddenly, he hears a muted conversation at the front of the office and recognizes Russling's voice, speaking with Mary. "Shit, what am I doing?" Gently he slides the drawer closed, picks up the trash bin from beside the desk and goes to exit. Mike is nearly to the doorway when the silhouette of Sheriff Russling blocks the office entrance.

A heavy, thick-framed man, the sheriff wears his law-badge and gun as an extension of his unsympathetic nature. There is a long silence as he stands ominously at the entry. "What's going on, Mike?"

The newly-appointed deputy can't help but revert to his teenage years, and the sense of unease created from his first meeting with Russling. "Nothing..." Mike looks down at the wastepaper bin. "Just emptying the trash."

The Sheriff stares intensely at Mike and seems to intuitively sense his primal nervousness. He looks down at the waste-paper can in Mike's hand and then glimpses to the outer office where the police file folders are placed on the deputy's desk. "Last night, I grabbed those files off your desk on the graffiti kids."

Mike stands uneasy in the middle of the sheriff's office and nods his head. "I noticed they were missing."

Russling blows out a snuffle of breath through his nostrils, contemplating, and responds, "Hope you don't mind. I had something real special, to teach them a proper lesson."

Unable to exit the uncomfortable conversation or the sheriff's office because of his blocked escape, Mike shifts his feet and replies, "I thought it was one of the very few things in my department?"

Cicada

The sheriff gives a wolfish grin and narrows his eyes. "When it requires a special kind of justice, it falls into mine."

Mike nods with subordination and moves to exit the office. "Okay, that's fine... Excuse me."

Sheriff Russling remains in the doorway and doesn't budge or shift aside to let the new deputy pass. His dark eyes scrutinize Mike, making the encounter even more awkward. "I saw some other file reports, just now, over on your desk. What are you looking into?"

Mike stands, holding the trash bin before him and attempts to meet the sheriff's firm gaze. "Nothing much, really... I was just going over some of the old case files, getting familiar with my hometown again."

Sheriff Russling continues to study Mike for a second, and then he steps aside to finally let him pass by. "Sure... That's a good thing. I'm glad to see you're taking an interest." The sheriff's keen eye notices the new deputy's nervous perspiration and then drops to the tensely-gripped trash can. "Let me know if I can help with anything."

Mike's gaze connects briefly with Russling, and he slips out of the sheriff's sanctum. "Yeah... Sure. I'll let you know."

Chapter 8

Seventeen years prior ...

A late-sixties model Chevy Camaro drives slowly with its headlights beaming down a long, dark farm-to-market road. The loose gravel crunches under the tires and ghosting wisps of dust rise up from the tracks. Illuminated by the dashboard, John sits behind the steering wheel of the car and looks out the windshield into the night.

Ahead, the beacon of a security light on a tall power-pole casts a green, beam of light over a double-wide trailer. Around the mobile home, several cars are parked in the yard. John drives forward along the gravel roadway and turns at the narrow, rutted driveway leading to the house trailer and mix of abandoned automobiles.

As the car rolls down the driveway, John can see the glow from a table lamp and the television set inside the trailer. A strange tingling of nervousness fills John's stomach, so he takes deep, inhaling breaths to chase away his intoxication. Killing the engine and headlights, he looks at the junked automobiles surrounding his friend's home, and chuckles. "Damn... I should have borrowed a car from Mike."

The car's hot engine ticks, as John swings the door open and steps into the far-reaching glow of the security lighting. With a soft click, he closes the car door and works his way through the lot of parked cars to the front stoop of the trailer. At the entry door, in the shadows cast from the yard light, John tries to read the time on his watch and finally knocks.

John listens to the shuffling sounds of someone moving around inside. The volume clicks down on the television set. In the darkness, he tries to peer at his wristwatch again, as the light above the porch flicks on, momentarily blinding him. The door to the trailer opens and Mike's mom, Mrs. Connolly appears, looking exceptionally nice for a Friday night at home. In her late forties, she has a sexual aura about her that, rather than fading with the years, has added to her attractiveness. Outfitted in a white, form fitting t-shirt and worn-faded jeans, she is a remarkably good-looking woman.

Taking a moment to recognize each other, they both hesitate under the bright bulb of the buzzing, porch light. Awkwardly, John blurts out, like an elementary school-kid, "Hello, Miss Connolly!"

Her own set of drink-glazed eyes brighten with sudden recognition and she stares at him, surprised. "I'll be damned! John Bratcher, how are you? Come on in."

Cicada

Mike's mother opens the door wider and moves aside, welcoming him into the trailer. John enters the familiar home of his childhood friend and looks around the living and kitchen area. "How are you, Mrs. Connolly? Is Mike around?"

Closing the door, Mike's mother adjusts the black bra strap under her shirt and smiles at her son's longtime friend. "John, you're making me feel really old. Call me Sarah, please. Would you like something to drink?"

She moves across the living room, picks up a partially-filled cocktail glass from the coffee table and finishes it off. John stands uneasily in the trailer entry and grins. "Uh, sure... Whatever you're having."

With the lonely clink of the remaining ice in her glass, Mrs. Connolly struts into the kitchen and prepares to make two more mixed drinks. She peers over the messy kitchen countertop to the living room area and smiles sweetly at John. "Sit down and tell me about your school. How's it going?"

John sits on the couch before the muted television set and nervously tries to keep from ogling the sexually suggestive spectacle of Mrs. Connolly preparing the drinks. "Uh, school is fine, so far. It's a lot of work."

Her bosom jiggles, as she vigorously uses the cocktail shaker while smiling warmly at her son's longtime friend. "Wow, you sound just like Michael. He's busy with some training projects at the Police Academy this weekend."

Rising to his feet, John self-consciously looks around. "He's not home this weekend?" Mrs. Connolly steps around the kitchen counter and offers John one of the mixed drinks. "No, but that doesn't mean that you can't fill me in on what you've been doing lately." She takes John by the arm and guides him over to sit down on the couch next to her.

~*~

Outside the Burlingview police station, Frank is so intoxicated that he can barely stand upright. He wavers as a squad car pulls up and shines the bright headlights on him. He squints into the blinding light and then cracks a smile, as he jogs around to the passenger-side door and swings it open. Deputy Dodds sits, watching, in the driver's seat, as the passenger settles in and pulls the door closed.

"Hey, Frank."

The police deputy has a friendly charm about him that appeals to the high school kids he coaches in various sports. Dodds sniffs at the rank scent of alcohol brought into the car and stares disbelievingly at Frank. "Shit, man! Did you have to get schnockered before you came along?"

Frank puts on his most innocent-looking face and smiles at Dodds. "I just had a few."

The deputy shakes his head and puts the car in reverse. "When they reek of booze like they've had as many as you, they usually ride in the back. Your good buddy, Tom, should know something about that."

The police car backs into the street, straightens out and drives forward to the corner. Frank blows into his hand to smell his beer breath and smirks, "Do you have any mints?"

Cicada

Deputy Dodds gives Frank an upset look and shakes his head with disappointed. "Just don't vomit or stink up my car too much! I sure hope it's a quiet night in town."

Chapter 9

In the trailer home, on the pillow-stuffed love-seat together, John and Mrs. Connolly watch a police show on the television. Lights flash, as a car chases another car through the streets. Both of their drinks sit on the coffee table in front of them, nearly finished. Mrs. Connolly goes to take another sip from her glass tumbler and rests it on her bended knee. She looks at John and smiles warmly. "You look tense… Move over here."

"How do you mean?"

Mike's mother sets her cocktail back on the table and swings her legs wide around behind John to straddle his back. She takes hold of his tense shoulders to massage them and they instantly tighten up even more with her rubbing touch. John sits frozen in naive bewilderment, as he feels his friend's mother sliding her cool hands over his back and shoulders. She laughs and digs the heel of her palm against his spine. "You're so tight. How does that feel…? Better?"

Eric H. Heisner

John takes a big gulp from his glass, and the strength of the drink gives him a shiver. The influence of the alcohol pulses through his body, and his back begins to relax under her soothing touch. He watches as the television show blinks to commercials. The loud chattering drone of cicadas outside overwhelms the quiet breaks between programs.

Mrs. Connolly puts both hands on John's shoulders, squeezes them gently and leans forward to whisper in his ear. "The locusts sure are loud tonight."

Goose flesh runs down his neck and all over his body and the hair on his arms stand erect. "Actually they're cicadas. The males vibrate a membrane to make that shrill chatter to attract the female insects for mating. Locust don't do that."

Mrs. Connolly wraps her arms around John tighter and continues to speak in a low voice, near the nape of his neck. "You college boys are so smart."

Across the living room, a mirror reflects the sight of John sitting on the love-seat, embraced by his friend's mother. He catches a glimpse of the disturbing image and looks away. The rubbing on his shoulders continues, and Mrs. Connolly softly whispers, "You seem all tensed up again... Just relax."

Croaking out feebly, John utters, "If I was any more relaxed, I'd wet myself."

Laughing unsurely, under her breath, Mrs. Connolly pushes back from John. "Do you need to use the bathroom?"

His drink in hand, John stands and looks behind at Mrs. Connolly, lying with her legs spread-wide on the

Cicada

couch. "Yes... Yes, I do." He takes a gulping swallow to finish off the rest of the cocktail and sets it back down on the coffee table. Mrs. Connolly casually touches her fingertips along the inner seam of her jeans. "You know where it's at."

~*~

In the small bathroom of the mobile home, John awkwardly tries to urinate while in an overly-excited state. Leaning forward, he puts his hand on the toilet tank and stands on his toes to angle the stream of urine into the bowl. "Damn! I'm gonna break it, or end up peeing in my own face." After shaking off several delayed spurts, he zips up the fly of his trousers and turns to wash his hands in the sink. He looks at himself sternly in the vanity mirror and murmurs aloud, "You're an idiot! She is just being nice."

John dries his wet hands on the nearby towel and looks to his blurred reflection again. He attempts to shake away the drunkenness and mutters, "About time for you to go, buddy." He points a gun-like finger at himself in the bathroom mirror and pretends to shoot.

~*~

The police squad car drives out beyond the light of the town's street lamps and down the dark, county highway. Frank sits in the passenger seat and stifles a low, belching rumble that bubbles up from down deep in his stomach. "Where we headed?"

"I have a few routine stops and check-ups to make outside of town for the sheriff."

"Knute's Woods?"

"Yep, that's one of them. Usually catch one or two couples making out in their cars or on the picnic benches." The deputy looks over at his passenger and gives a laugh. "Sometimes, a whole lot more."

Frank sits back and smiles drunkenly. "Groovy!"

Chapter 10

The pulsing sound of police sirens blare from the television set, as John comes down the hallway after using the bathroom. He spots Mrs. Connolly sitting forward at one end of the small love-seat and has a foolish notion. With intoxicated judgement, he decides to run the remaining few feet and leap over the back of the sofa, like actors do on car hoods in television shows. Intending to land seated, beside her, John's foot catches the top of the lampshade and instead, brings the fixture crashing down on top of Mrs. Connolly. "Ohh, shit…!"

His foot tangled in the power cord across her back, Mike's mother pushes the lamp from her shoulder and cries, "What the hell?"

John quickly tosses the broken lampshade aside to reveal a nasty-looking scrape under her torn shirt. "I'm sorry. Mrs. Connolly, are you alright?" John sets the broken lamp on the floor and stands nervously over her.

Eric H. Heisner

She looks up at him from the love-seat and arches her injured back. "Yeah, yeah... Nothing a few drinks can't fix." Touching her back, she winces and looks at traces of blood on her fingers. "What were you doing?"

At a loss for words, John feels momentarily sobered and stutters, "I, uh, I just..."

She takes John by the hand and pulls herself up from the low sofa seat. "Never mind. Help me get this cleaned up." Mrs. Connolly continues to hold his hand as she leads him to the kitchen.

John follows and apologizes. "I am really sorry."

She tows him along behind her and points to a recessed cabinet over the refrigerator. "It's okay. I have a first aid kit in that cupboard up there." Mrs. Connolly releases her hold of John's hand, and he reaches up to open the high cabinet door. Behind a prank-gift coffee mug reading: "World's Best Farter – I mean Father", next to a small fire-extinguisher, is a white box with a red first aid sign on the lid.

"Is that your coffee mug?" John immediately regrets bringing up the subject of Mike's missing father, takes out the first aid kit and puts it on the countertop. He is shocked to see Mrs. Connolly peel off her ripped t-shirt to reveal a black bra. She touches the wound on her back again and, without a moment's hesitation, she unclips her brassiere and slings it on the counter.

Her torso exposed, down to the top of her jeans, she opens the first aid kit and sorts through the creams and bandages. She looks up to see John gawking, dumbfounded, at her chest. "Stop staring at my tits, and help me clean this." She hands John a pad of cotton with some anti-bacterial cream on it and turns the scrape on her back toward him. He dabs the fresh cut and gently wipes the small smear of blood away.

Mrs. Connolly peeks over her exposed shoulder and observes John carefully doctoring the minor-scrape. She winces slightly, and he puts his hand to her arm. "Does it hurt?"

She holds onto his fingers and turns around to him. "Not anymore. Here, give me that."

They stand face to face under the bright kitchen light, as Mrs. Connolly takes his hand with the swab. She heaves her chest out, stepping closer, and John leans forward to plant a kiss on the lips of his friend's mother. There is a definite awkwardness with the encounter; John quickly stops and pulls away. "I am so sorry…"

Still grasping John's hand, she doesn't let him back away. Their eyes connect, hers showing a lustful, intoxicated yearning. She takes a step forward and urges him closer.

~*~

The dark outline of the police car crunches down a gravel drive. The headlights beam out to a wooded, public park ahead. Deputy Dodds rolls down the window and scans a handheld spotlight out across the unoccupied parking area. The extended wand of light travels across the brush at the base of the tree-line and lights up one of the trail marker signs.

Deputy Dodds pans the beam of light back again, and then clicks off the spotlight as he pulls it inside the car. "Nope, no luck tonight."

Perched in the front seat, Frank peers over the deputy's shoulder and sinks down, unimpressed with the results. "Damn... I wanted to see some sort of illicit action tonight."

Dodds shrugs, as he places the spotlight on the seat between them. "Sorry, you'll just have to wait for Sticky to drive home drunk, later tonight."

Deputy Dodds looks over his shoulder, shifts the car into reverse, and the engine whines as it goes backward. Frank puts his feet up on the dashboard and kicks back. "Where to now?"

The deputy lets the car roll to a stop and shifts into the forward gear. "One more place to check out before heading back to town." The police car swings around, spitting gravel as it tears off down the lane.

Chapter 11

The only light in the double-wide trailer comes from the main living area. Reflected off the front, wide-glass window, the flickering glow of the television set lights up the room. Oblivious to the laughing sounds of some late night talk show, two naked bodies embrace on the couch, kissing and fondling.

~*~

On a rural two-lane highway, the Burlingview Police car drives through the darkness of night. The dashboard instruments light up the features of the deputy as he drives. Frank looks over at Dodds and then out to the stretch of empty highway illuminated before them. "What's out here? You're not going to murder me and leave me in a ditch somewhere are you?"

The deputy smiles and his eyes twinkle playfully. "Who would notice if I did?"

Exaggerating an audible swallow, Frank turns to the passenger door and play-acts vigorously yanking on the handle. "Let me out of here, you degenerate psycho! Heeelp!"

Dodds gazes over at Frank and laughs with him, "Just one quick stop. I have to check-in on something."

~*~

Inside the isolated trailer-home, two glistening, nude bodies heave against each other. Through the front bay-window, the headlights of the police squad car can be seen as they stop at the end of the long driveway and switch off. For a long while, the police car sits still in the starlit dimness.

~*~

Deputy Dodds watches the blue flicker of the late-night television program, as it lights up and reflects off the front bay-window of the trailer-home. He glances at Frank, beside him playing with a pair of handcuffs. The deputy rests his wrist over the steering wheel, as he continues to watch the window. "Looks like all is well."

Frank turns to the deputy and seems very confused. "Part of your routine is to check on Mike's mom's place?" Dodds turns to his passenger and smirks, "Yeah, shit-brain. Russling lives there now, too." There is a crackle on the radio, and the deputy turns down the volume control and shrugs. "He just wanted me to swing by and check while he's away." Dodds drops his hand from the steering wheel to the keys dangling from the ignition. He is about the turn them, when Mrs. Connolly's unclothed figure pops up in the window, taking a suggestive sitting position.

Frank is nearly beside himself with excited delight. "Holy-shit...! Hot-damn, did you see that?"

Cicada

Dodds drops his hand from the ignition key and his jaw slacks as he murmurs, "Yes … Yes, I did."

"Mike's mom is definitely a MILF."

"A what?"

"M.I.L.F., you know, Mom I'd like to…"

"Yeah, yeah! Shut up a minute."

"Why? What's going on."

"Just shut up, and let me think!"

Deputy Dodds brings out a small flashlight, which he shines on the various license plates of the cars parked around the trailer-home. He spots an out-of-state plate and clicks off the light. Frank is wide-eyed and can't take his gaze off the electronic glow against the arching form appearing again in the window. "I thought you said the sheriff wasn't home?"

Scribbling the out-of-state license plate number down on a notepad, Dodds shakes his head unhappily. "He's not." The police deputy looks at his passenger in all seriousness. "You have to keep quiet. I have to get the sheriff on the radio."

In the dim interior of the car, Frank glows a pale white. "Sheriff Russling?" They both realize the gravity of the situation, and Frank mutters, "What the hell are you going to tell him? Someone is screwing his wife on the couch?"

The deputy shakes his head and sneaks another glimpse at the strobing blue light of the television coming through the living room window and starts up the squad car. "No, but I need to check in, and I have to tell him something." He puts the car in reverse and creeps backward down the road until they are a short distance away from the driveway entrance, but can still see the parked cars and trailer-home. "He's expecting a call from me tonight, at about this time." Dodds brings the police car to a stop and looks over at Frank. "I will need you to get out of the vehicle while I radio this in." The nervous passenger nods silently and quietly pulls the door handle to exit.

~*~

Two bodies lie clenched in each other's arms on the love-seat sofa. The glowing flicker from the late-night television program continues to put an intermittent light on their embracing forms. On the trailer-home's shag carpet floor, scattered articles of piled clothing and a broken lamp set the illicit scene.

~*~

Inside the squad car, the deputy puts down the radio and motions through the window for Frank to get back in. Frank slips in the front passenger side and gently clicks the door closed. "Did you tell him? What did the sheriff say?"

Dodds looks quite grim and unsettled as he responds, "He said to watch the house and the car until he gets here."

Frank seems taken aback. "He's coming here, now?" The interior of the police vehicle is deathly quiet as Deputy Dodds nods. Frank squirms in his seat and looks to the trailer off in the distance. "What do you think he's gonna do?"

Dodds lowers his chin and stares at the steering wheel. "I don't know. When I told him about the car in the driveway, he got worked up and said he was coming right away."

"I thought the police convention he is attending is an overnight thing a few hours away, in the city or something?"

The police deputy nods solemnly, "It is."

Chapter 12

Mike sits back in his chair, looking some papers over. He rubs his forehead, then carefully slips the file report papers back into the slim manila folder on his desk. Hearing the front door open, Mike looks up to see Frank enter the police station.

With no one seated at the front reception area, Frank walks directly to Mike's desk. "You wanted to see me, Mike?" Frank, unshaven and dressed in oil-stained mechanic overalls, after years of manual labor, has lost his boyish features and youthful exuberance.

Mike lets his chair rock forward and, with a welcoming smile, he looks Frank over. "Yeah, I was just thinking about us and the good old times we used to have in school."

Somewhat ill at ease, Frank glances around the police station, letting his gaze linger on the sheriff's office door. "Don't hurt yerself thinking about it too much… Not all of them were that good."

Mike notices the direction of Frank's stare and turns to look over his shoulder to the darkened doorway. He considers asking him about his interest in the sheriff's office but instead smiles kindly to his old friend. "What have you been up to, Frank?"

"Same shit, just a different day." The car mechanic holds up his permanently grease-stained hands before wiping his palms on his pants legs.

Mike stacks the files on his desk and puts them aside before turning his attention to his old friend. "I know what you mean. The most exciting thing in the last few weeks around here has been setting up my desk."

"Dangerous stuff."

"Only the highly-trained experts survive."

Frank finally cracks a faint smile, seems to let his guard down, and then looks around the old police station again. "Yeah, I bet it's a change from working in the big city."

"It sure is."

"What did you come back for?"

Mike straightens the front of his uniform shirt and leans back in the chair. He peers up at Frank standing across the desk from him and shrugs. "To be closer to my mother." The deputy glances around the empty police station fondly. "Thought maybe I could make a difference somewhere? It can be real scary back there, feeling like you're just a part of their system. I wanted to be more involved with the community... Kinda like my dad was."

The mention of Mike's dad turns Frank's gaze, and he shifts his stance. "Hear from him any?"

Cicada

"Naw. Don't expect to anymore." The clean desktop shines under the fluorescent lights, as Mike sweeps his hand over the smooth surface. "You know who I *was* thinking about?"

"Nope."

"John."

Frank suddenly looks like he just took a sucker-punch directly to the gut. "Who?"

"John Bratcher."

The mechanic takes another nervous glance around the police station, attempting to conceal his stunned reaction. "Jeez! What the hell for?"

"I thought I saw him today."

Not sure what to think or how to respond, Frank stares at the police deputy. "What the hell are you talking about?"

Mike leans forward in his chair and puts his forearms to the edge of the desk. He pauses, and then whispers jokingly to his old pal, "Have you seen him?"

Visually disturbed, Frank fidgets with the pocket flap on his coveralls and replies, "No."

"Yeah, guess not. I'm not even sure if I have either. He's just another one of this town's many ghost stories now."

The silence is deafening as the two friends stare at each other from across the desktop. Frank breaks the standstill. "What was it again I needed to come down here for? I really hate it around here."

"Sit down." Mike observes as Frank once again uneasily looks to the sheriff's office door before pulling up a chair to sit. He looks across the desk to his former schoolmate and asks, curiously, "Why is that?"

"Why's what?"

Mike shrugs his shoulders and leans back in the chair. "You would always love coming around when we were kids. In high school, we were here all the time."

Frank shifts uncomfortably in his chair and grunts. "Guess you grow out of some things."

"How's the garage? You own it now, don't you?"

"It's fine. You know… The same."

"You busy?"

Frank folds and laces his dark-stained fingers together, obviously not wanting to be there. "It has always been steady. If it has wheels and rolls down the road, it'll break down."

Mike rocks his chair back slightly and tries to keep the uncomfortable conversation upbeat. "Do you remember in school, when our track team went to the State Championships?"

Frank nods and forces a grin, "Yeah, I was on the baseball team though."

"Oh yeah, I forgot." Mike notices how Frank keeps a paranoid ear toward the front office entrance and can't seem to help but continue glancing around the empty police station. He calls his friend out on the odd behavior. "What are you looking for?"

Frank turns to John and fakes a friendly smile. "Nothing… I just forgot what this place looked like."

Swiveling a bit to the side in his chair, Mike nods. "Since I started, it's only been me, Russling and Mary.

Cicada

Usually quiet around here, most of the time. For some reason, he sure goes through the deputies."

A cold chill rises from the pit of Frank's stomach, and he wipes his dry forehead. "What do you mean?"

"I don't know. They probably get bored as hell and move on to someplace more interesting than Burlingview." Glancing at the file folders on his desk, Mike thinks a minute. "You were pretty good friends with that Deputy Dodds, weren't you?"

Frank nods and anxiously clears his throat. "Yeah. I just knew him as one of the coaches."

"How was it you got to know Dodds?"

"I dunno… He was a coach."

Mike tries not to put on an interrogating tone but still pushes the questioning further. "Yeah… But, he coached track and field in the springtime, and you were doing baseball." Frank pauses a second and then replies, "I played softball with him on the weekends."

"I remember you used to come down here a lot, when he was the new deputy and my dad was still the sheriff in town."

"I guess so."

"What happened?"

Frank doesn't appreciate the unofficial grilling and stares at Mike. "I don't know… I just lost interest."

Mike thinks a moment and then shrugs, trying to keep the conversation friendly. "Well, if you ever want to go on a ride along, let me know."

Frank doesn't respond.

"Nothing ever happens, but it's nice to have the company along."

Seated stiffly in the chair, Frank turns pale and starts to sweat as he shifts both his hands on the armrests to stand. "What was it you wanted to talk to me about?"

"You know, I can't even remember exactly. Wasn't anything really important... I just wanted to catch up with you some." As Frank rises from the chair, Mike looks up at his old classmate and smiles. "Want to grab a beer tonight with the other guys at Hall's Tap? Maybe I'll remember what it was."

Frank scoots the chair back with his legs and shakes his head. "Not tonight. Have to help the wife out at the house."

He moves over to the door, as Mike calls out after him. "Maybe some other time?"

Frank glances back and gives a wave. "Yeah sure. Say hello to Mary."

The front door of the police station swings open and Frank quickly exits. Mike pulls out a pad of paper from his desk drawer and scribbles down some notes. He thinks quietly and then pulls a box of still-to-be-unpacked supplies from alongside his desk.

Digging through the cardboard file box, he comes out with a vintage police badge which reads: *Sheriff M. Connolly*. Mike rubs the engraved details with his fingertips and slides it into the breast pocket of his police uniform. He digs deeper in the box and finds a small voice recorder, then opens it to check that there is a cassette tape loaded inside.

Mike coughs, clearing his throat and uses an attempted 'Joe Friday' detective-style voice as he presses the record tab.

Cicada

"The unsolved murder case of the John Bratcher disappearance. Gone missing and supposedly killed seventeen years ago by an itinerant drifter. When, why, and where did the body go? Who in town actually knows anything? Frank seems to know something... Where are you John Bratcher?"

Chapter 13

The center through-street and town square of Burlingview is peaceful and quiet as Mike walks down the empty sidewalk. He scans the vacant storefronts and few remaining businesses, observing the dull serenity of a small town, past its prime. Strolling leisurely through the downtown, Mike walks toward *Aunt Missy's Homecookin' Diner*.

A full-figured, older woman exits the diner's glass door with a corn broom in hand. Aunt Missy Raymond has a vivacity and life-spark energy to her that even the lethargy of small town living can't quell. A warm smile spreads across Mikes features at the sight of her sweeping the sidewalk. "Hello, Missus Raymond."

The aproned woman spins on her broom handle like a puffy enchantress doing a U-turn. Her jowls spread wide to a charming smile that make her deep-set eyes almost twinkle. "Well, hello there, Mister Deputy."

Eric H. Heisner

Stopping at the front of the eatery, Mike laughs and seems to revert to being just one of the neighborhood kids. "You don't have to call me that."

Missy laughs and looks him over in his new police uniform. "Since when do you call me Missus Raymond, sweetie-pie?"

"I guess it's been too long a time since I've been home. It's good to see you, Aunt Missy."

The wide, vivacious woman sweeps the broom handle between them and a leaf lifts and swirls away to the street. "It's all that high struttin' big city life frying your brain 'nstead of yer bacon 'n biscuits, with its hustlin' and bustle." An automobile drives down the street, and Mike watches the driver slow and gives a friendly wave toward Aunt Missy. She returns the gesture, looks at Mike and titters with glee. "Speakin' of the city life, this is the rush hour 'round here."

Mike smiles and peers inside the diner at the few eating. "I guess I don't have to worry about traffic."

The café owner catches his derogatory remark, pauses and then continues her purposeless sweeping. "Most of us like it that way around here. It's been that way for a long time. We'd just as soon have it quiet and be left alone."

"That is all there seems to be... Quiet."

She turns her ear to the town and smiles big. "Nice, huh?"

Mike gazes down the empty, wide-open street and wonders if the town center was ever really prosperous and if all the storefronts were occupied. "It's a small, dying town."

Cicada

Missy casts a reproachful glance at the deputy. "Big enough… Some folks spend their whole lives trying to get out, and others can't help but come back."

Understanding her implication, Mike takes a breath. "When is the last time something did happen around here?"

"In Burlingview?"

"Yeah."

"Why?"

"Just curious."

Aunt Missy looks up at him with a questioning eye before looking down at an empty insect shell on the sidewalk. "Boy, them little cicada bugs sure do leave a nasty carcass. You ever think how funny it is how that one little thing sure can fix up a heap of racket?" She sweeps the bug to the curb. "Hell, most folks only care when I change the menu on them." Missy continues sweeping and looks at Mike. "You know how to move a church piano?

Mike lifts an eyebrow and shakes his head. "Nope."

The broom swishes across the pavement and the woman chuckles, "One inch at a time." She gives Mike a wink. "When something does happen around here, most soon forget 'cause it's best not to get your nose stuck in others' business." Missy takes hold of her own nose and gives it a wiggle.

The street remains mostly quiet, and Mike gazes out into the lonesomeness of the small country town. "Not everyone forgets."

Missy bends down and picks up an old penny from the curb. She rubs it a few times, looks at the year and murmurs, "That's lucky", before slipping it into her front apron pocket. Her attentions return to Mike and her sweeping, as she tilts her head empathetically. "Nope, but we like to let things be."

The conversation lulls, while she sweeps a few wisps of dust from the curb into the street. Reflecting on his childhood, Mike sighs, "When Dad was the sheriff, no one had to forget."

Pausing her sweeping, Aunt Missy leans on her broom handle and the bristles crackle under the weighted strain. "Naw, it was sure different alright. You was young though, and everything looked good to you." Missy looks down the street and back at Mike. "Sometimes different is just the same in a different way." She flashes a smile and another wink in Mike's direction, adjusting her leaning stance with the broom. "Don't you go lookin' to change things too much, sweetie. You settle in and raise a few pups for me to spoil, okay?"

Mike salutes jokingly. "Yes, ma'am!"

"Don't you 'Yes ma'am' me, Mister!"

Unable to resist Aunt Missy's warm, generous spirit, Mike smiles at her and nods. "I'll be seeing you around, Missus Raymond." He resumes his patrol walk down the street, and Missy, continuing her sweeping, calls out, "Alrighty there, Mister Deputy... Take care!"

~*~

Through the partly shuttered blinds of the police station, the afternoon brightness of day begins its fading glow. Mike sits in his chair under the fluorescent lights of the office, fiddling with the writing pad and voice recorder on his lap. He looks around the office and glances at Russling's door.

Mike's desk chair creaks back, breaks the silence, and he stands. Taking a few steps toward the station entrance, he looks around the corner to Mary's empty receptionist chair. He looks behind to the sheriff's glass paneled office door and moves toward it.

Finding the door unlocked, Mike cracks it open and peers into the shady interior. Beaming rays of sunlight slant through the closed blinds, casting bars of light across the floor. Mike gazes around the Sheriff's inner sanctuary and glances over his shoulder briefly before slipping inside.

Chapter 14

The top, middle drawer on the sheriff's desk quietly slides open, and Mike grabs up the metal ring with two small keys. He goes to the file cabinet and slips one of them into the lock. A quick turn of the key and the locking tab clicks out to unlock the drawer. Pausing for a moment, Mike listens to the empty silence of the office.

Only hesitating briefly, Mike pulls open the first drawer and peers inside, as he carefully thumbs through the names at the top of the files. Not finding anything of interest, he quietly closes the metal drawer and opens the next. Halfway down the row of stacked files, Mike pauses on a folder labeled: *Bratcher, John - unsolved*. He pulls the file sleeve, spreads it out on the open drawer and scans the report inside. He reads aloud: *John A. Bratcher... missing, presumed to be dead*. Mike turns the report page over and starts reading the next. Scanning halfway down the paperwork another name catches his eye: *Hank Simms, murder/assault suspect – See file*.

Mike closes the file on John Bratcher and thumbs through the file cabinet drawer again. He pulls out another folder that reads: *Simms, Hank.* Scanning over the file report, Mike pauses on the page that logs the booking fingerprints. His studied eye wanders the circumstances leading to the inked marks until his gaze comes to rest on the booking date. He quickly reopens John Bratcher's case file and compares the information with the date of the incident.

"If Hank Simms was involved with John disappearing, why would he be booked days before?"

He flips back a few pages in the police report, until a noise at the entrance of the station breaks his concentration. Hairs rise on the back of his neck, as Mike quickly tucks the inspected files back in the drawer, slides it closed and locks it. He moves behind the big desk in the room, replaces the keys in the center drawer and moves to the door. He looks outside to the empty police station and exits the inner office doorway, quietly closing the sheriff's door behind him.

Out in the main office, Mike looks around and listens. Only the electric hum from the overhead bulbs can be heard. "Is anyone here?"

There is a long, eerie silence that is broken by the tapping of a heavy foot on the tiled floor by the front entry. Mike walks around the corner to find Sheriff Russling perusing some papers spread out across Mary's desktop. He looks up at Mike. "Find anything new?"

"Uh... No."

The sheriff puts Mary's papers down, shuffles them back into the original pile, and moves past Mike to his office. He stops midway, hesitates, and then turns to face the deputy. "Hey Mike, it's pretty slow this afternoon. Why don't you do the rounds and go home. I'll call you if anything comes up."

Mike watches, as the sheriff deliberately scans his desk as he passes through the station. He looks to the squad car outside and calls to Russling, who is about to enter his office. "I thought I might get some more done."

Russling holds his office door open, flips on the light and peers back at Mike. "Don't worry about it. You'll have time for it tomorrow. Go on, get out of here."

The sheriff enters his office and closes the door behind. Mike goes to his desk and grabs his car keys, writing notebook and voice recorder. He glances at Russling's private office, with the closed blinds, and slides the general office files on John Bratcher between the pages of his notebook.

~*~

There is a grinding crunch of gravel, as the police car drives along a country road and turns down a narrow lane. Parked at the end of the driveway are several junked cars and a mobile-home trailer. Mike stops the squad car behind one of the abandoned vehicles and swings his door open to step out. He stands and looks at the stationary trailer-home with a yard security light mounted on the tall power pole.

There is a gentle knock at the trailer-home door before it opens, and Mike steps into the dim, curtain-drawn interior. "Mother...? Mom, you home?" Mike moves to the kitchen and helps himself to some leftover food still out on the counter.

Eric H. Heisner

The shuffling of slippers is heard, and Mrs. Connolly comes down the hallway in her bedroom attire and robe. "What's going on Mike? The invite to come over for dinner was for tomorrow evening."

Opening the refrigerator, Mike grabs from the limited selection of canned beer and walks around to the living room. He sits on the couch and looks across the coffee table at the full-console television set. "Mother, I know its for tomorrow. I just had a rough day and wanted to talk to you."

Mrs. Connolly seems to be nursing a late afternoon hangover, as she eases herself into a chair across from Mike. "A rough day in Burlingview? What happened, someone get arrested and hauled into the hoosegow for not using the crosswalk?"

Mike pops the top open on the beer and takes a swig. He sits forward, looks at the floor and then up at his mother. "What would you say if I said I ran into John Bratcher today?"

The rosy complexion seems to drain from Mrs. Connolly's face as she braces herself on the arm of the chair. "What do you mean?"

Mike reluctantly confides to his mother, worried that she might think he's crazy. "I don't think John is really dead... Just missing."

In disbelief, she stares at Mike as a wave of panic briefly passes over her. "What are you talking about?"

Observing her odd reaction, Mike uneasily continues, "My friend, John Bratcher... You remember him, don't you?"

Cicada

Feeling the need for a strong drink to chase away her mounting angst, Mrs. Connolly tries to avoid eye contact with her son. "What about him?"

"I think he's alive."

The urge for a drink becomes overwhelming for Mrs. Connolly, despite her recent hangover. "That's just ridiculous. It happened so many years ago. Wouldn't he have turned up already by now?"

"Not if he's hiding."

"Hiding from what?"

"I don't know."

"How much have you had to drink today?"

"How much have you?"

"Michael!"

Mike tilts his head and takes a drink from the beer. He muses aloud, "There has got to be something." Mike watches with concern, as Mrs. Connolly shakily gets up from her chair. "Are you okay, Mother?"

Having had enough of the conversation, she waves him away and places her fingertips against her temples to rub out the throbbing pain. "It was probably just something I ate." The empty cocktail tumblers left around the room tell a different story, and Mrs. Connolly shuffles to the kitchen to make another drink. She fixes herself a double and stares at her son. "Who says he's in hiding, Michael?"

Mike is reluctant to tell her more but, since he has no one else to confide in, he relents. "I think I saw him."

As she takes a swallow from her drink, his mother seems to regain a bit of color. "What did he say?"

Eric H. Heisner

Standing from the couch, Mike walks to his mother in the kitchen and tentatively answers, "He didn't say anything. I didn't get to speak with him."

"Why not?"

Mike begins to show obvious frustration with having his closest confidant not seem to believe him. "He's in *hiding*. He didn't stick around to chat with me."

Mrs. Connolly finishes off her drink and pours another one before walking back to the living room. She adjusts her bathrobe, and shuffles past her son as she shakes her head. "You're scaring me, Michael. Do you need a doctor or a therapist to talk to?" Gripping her drink, she takes a seat.

Obviously hurt by her complete lack of understanding, Mike puts his beer down. "I'm fine."

Looking up at him from the chair, Mrs. Connolly seems glassy-eyed already. "No, you're not. You said you saw someone who's been dead for twenty years."

"More like seventeen, and, only presumed dead."

"Okay, and once you stay that way long enough, it's usually best to leave it alone." She takes a short sip from her drink and sets it down.

Mike shifts over and sits across from her. "I saw him today, and I'm going to find out why."

She looks away, unable to make eye contact with her son. "Whatever you're doing, I don't want to be involved."

"You already are. The whole town is."

When Mrs. Connolly tries to stand, Mike puts his hand on her leg and presses her back down to sit. Despite the easy touch, Mrs. Connolly immediately overreacts like she is being forcefully restrained, "Michael!"

He removes his hand and speaks firmly with his mom. "I need to know what happened the night John disappeared. Did he call here or stop by?

"I don't know." She grabs her cocktail from the side table and takes a long sip, looking deep into the glass tumbler.

Mike watches her with a growing frustration, knowing she will soon be drunk again. "Before you were attacked that night, what really happened? Did anyone call or stop by?" Mike senses his mother's turmoil, as he gazes into her eyes. "Did you visit anyone in town that day? Who did you see?" Mike studies his mother's reaction and he continues. "What happened that night?"

Mrs. Connolly's eyelids close for a moment, as she slowly wobbles her head and murmurs, "I can't remember, dammit. Go read the damn police reports."

Mike shakes his head. "It's not in the reports."

"I can't…"

Unsatisfied with his mom's response, Mike presses on. "Did you know Hank Simms? Did he possibly know John…?" Mike stares into the glazed eyes of his mother. "Please tell me what happened, mother. It's important!"

The two sit silently, until the sound of an approaching vehicle is heard, crunching its way up the gravel driveway. Mrs. Connolly springs to her feet and looks out the window. "He's home."

Mike watches his mother's strangely terrified reaction as she stands to look out the front bay windows.

"Who knew Simms?" He gets up and moves close to her. "Think about it. I need to know, so I can find him."

The door swings open, and Sheriff Russling enters. Stepping into the trailer-home, he smirks when he sees Mike stand between him and his wife, as if he needs to protect her. "Hello Mike. Is this where you go and spend your time off? Staying for supper?"

Mike looks from his mother to Russling. "No, I uh… Just stopped by to visit with my mom." He moves to the door, and Russling steps out of his way.

"Mike, you're looking awful upset and serious of late. Is the new job getting the better of you?"

"No. Just a lot on my mind."

"Well, don't worry about it anymore."

As the Sheriff grins, Mike asks, "Why's that?"

"There is no use getting worked up over nothing." Trying to make out his true meaning, Mike stares at Russling, but only receives a smug expression.

"I'll try not to." With a strange, uneasy feeling, Mike exits the doorway of his mother's trailer and returns to his car.

Chapter 15

The local watering hole, Hall's Tap, has a consistent crowd of regulars that habitually comes to drink its fill every night. Mike, in civilian clothing, enters the tavern and is greeted with a few reluctant gazes. He moves up to the bar and orders a beer from the large man behind the counter, Sammy.

The friendly bartender looks Mike up and down before offering a sociable smile. "Haven't seen you in a while, Mike. Where you been hiding?"

Mike shrugs and glances around the barroom full of people he recognizes from the town. He notices that several acquaintances seem to avoid eye contact. "It doesn't look good for the new deputy in town to go around getting shit-faced on the weekends."

Sammy pops open a can of beer. He slides it to Mike and puts an elbow to the bar. "I'll stop you when you get to dancing on tables or shooting people. Good to see you again."

Mike watches Sammy work his way down the counter, and notices Frank with a group of his friends at the far end. Their eyes meet for a moment before Frank averts his gaze. Mike takes a sip of his beer, sets it down on the bar and moves through the crowd toward Frank.

Seeing Mike make his way over, Frank gets up to leave. As off-duty deputy approaches his old group of friends, Frank stares suspiciously at Mike. "What are you doing here?"

Mike smiles, and can't help but notice that Frank hasn't been home yet, as he is still in his dirty work clothes from the garage. "Thought you had to help out the wife tonight?"

Frank falters for comment, until Chris and Tom turn on their bar chairs to see who he is talking to. Nearly falling from his perch, Chris lifts his beer from the bar and blurts out, "Holy shit! It's the future Sheriff!"

Tom spins on his padded stool and grins at Mike. "Dang, Mike! Where the hell did you finally crawl out from?" Mike momentarily turns his attention away from Frank and greets his old, high school buddies. "Hey! How are you guys? I should have figured you'd still be hanging 'round this guy." Frank responds awkwardly to Mike's friendly nudge.

Leaning his elbows back on the bar rail, his hand wrapped around a can of beer, Chris grins wide and snorts. "What finally brings your ass here? Official police business?" He takes a long swig of beer and continues to smile at Mike. "We haven't seen you around at all since you started working for this shit-hole of a town."

Cicada

Mike shrugs a reply, "Just busy getting settled in with the new job."

Tom twists his bottom back and forth on the barstool, making it creak, and laughs. "Trying to be upstanding and respectable or something?"

Chris takes another drink from his beer and looks to Mike's empty hands. "Hey, let me buy you a drink."

Mike raises his empty palm and looks around, amazed. "I did have one somewhere around here. I'll be right back." He turns back to the other end of the bar and goes to retrieve his drink.

As they watch Mike go, Frank tosses a few dollars on the bar top. "Alright, I'll see you guys later."

Surprised, Chris pulls his chin back and grimaces at Frank. "What your deal? He said he'd be right back."

Tom stops swiveling his chair and plants his feet on the floor. "Where you going?"

Without another word to his friends, Frank heads for the back door of the tavern intending to slip out to the alley. Mike returns with his beer just as the door to the exit closes. He looks first to his two friends and then past them to the empty spot at the bar where the crumpled dollars remain. "Where's Frank?"

Chris nods his head toward the back door. "Fuckin' weird-man just left."

~*~

The rear exit door of Hall's Tap bursts wide open, and Mike steps outside to look around. He spots Frank halfway down the alleyway and moves to catch up with him, calling out, "Frank! Hold on there a minute."

Eric H. Heisner

Pretending not to hear anything, the mechanic continues walking away from the bar. "Frank! Wait up…"

Frank turns his head slightly as he hears Mike behind, jogging nearer. He halts and pauses before turning around. He watches the town deputy slow to a walk and approach. "Mike, I've got to get home."

Taking a breath to catch his air, Mike stops in front of Frank. "What's going on with you?"

"What do you mean?"

"Frank, you've been avoiding me for a long time, and now you're going to lie to me too?"

"Screw you."

Frank turns to leave, and Mike follows along after him. From a few steps behind, he talks to the backside of Frank. "What the hell happened?"

"I don't know what you're talking about."

"Between us, Frank… What happened?"

When Mike reaches out to give Frank a friendly shove, the mechanic spins violently around and takes a swing at him. The punch merely glances off Mike's shoulder but, rightfully, startles him. On the defensive, Frank stares at Mike with a troubled anger in his eyes. "Mike, get the hell away from me!" His fists raised, Frank glares threateningly at the deputy. "Unless you're arresting me for something, just stay away." Frank slowly takes a step back, turns and keeps walking.

Startled by the unexpected outburst of resentment, Mike watches Frank walk away down the dimly-lit alleyway. "We're going to talk, Frank." The mechanic doesn't break pace or respond, as he moves into the shadows and disappears around the corner.

Chapter 16

Inside the crowded barroom, Tom downs the remainder of his beer and picks up his next one, from the lineup on the bar. He smiles and clanks his bottle on Mike's almost empty can. "Can't wait until you're the sheriff."

The deputy laughs and looks to his beer, mentally measuring the time left in it. "Why's that?"

Chris leans in and pipes up with a disapproving grunt. "This dumbass thinks he won't get thrown in jail anymore for public intoxication and passing out drunk on the sidewalk."

Tom gives his buddy Chris a queer expression and then turns to Mike. "I won't, will I?"

Mike finishes off his beer and sets it in line on the bar. "It's a tough call on that one. We'll see… I have to get going." Mike takes one last look around at the people in the bar still avoiding his gaze. "It was good hanging with you guys."

Chris reaches out and pats Mike on the shoulder. "Good to see you again, too. Sorry 'bout Frank, though."

"Why are you sorry about Frank?"

Chris exchanges a peculiar look with Tom, shrugs and almost looks regretful about mentioning anything to Mike. "Aw, he's been so weird about you for a while. Who knows?"

Mike stands before his high school friends trying hard not to shift into interrogation mode. "Since when?"

"I dunno, since you moved back." Tom spins around on his bar stool while holding his beer bottle on his knee. "Naw, the fucker's been mental since John disappeared."

Mike shifts his gaze to the rear exit door of the tavern and then back at his friends. "Yeah?"

Looking troubled, Chris shrugs. "Hasn't been easy for any of us, but life goes on just the same. Didn't click with Frank though, I guess."

They all are reverently quiet until Mike breaks the uncomfortable pause. "You saw him that night, didn't you?"

Chris lifts his can of beer from the bar and asks, "Who... John?" He takes a drinks and nods to Mike. "You would have too, if you had come home for a visit that weekend."

"He came in here?"

Tom clanks his beer bottle on the leg of the stool, between his knees, and nods his head. "He was headed out to your place when he ran into that Simms guy."

"Out to my mother's place?"

Cicada

Tom lifts the bottle to his chest and takes a drink before he responds, "I guess that's how they figured it went down."

Chris holds his fresh can of beer in his hand and looks to it fondly. "He did have quite a few drinks with Frank and us before he headed off to find you."

Tom grins at Chris and glances over his right shoulder. "I think he might have stuck around even longer if Mary hadn't spooked him.

Chris wobbles his head and rolls his eyes. "Damn… Don't ever let her hear you say that. Mary is the only one who took it harder than Frank did."

Mike's thoughts are muddled as he assesses the bits of information on John's disappearance. He looks to his beer can on the bar and flicks it with his finger. "I have to get going… I'll see you guys another time."

Tom spins on his stool as he finishes his beer and sets the empty bottle on the bar. He raises his hand to get the bartender's attention and waves over another round of drinks. "Sammy, another one for me and Chris."

Mike pushes his empty beer can back across the bar top and turns to leave. "It was sure good to see you both again."

Somewhat hesitant, Chris speaks up to stop him. "Mike… Don't take it personal about Frank. He feels guilty about not being there for Dodds, and I guess for John too."

With a puzzled expression, Mike turns to face Chris. "What do you mean about Dodds?"

Now even more reluctant, Chris glances at Tom but only receives a shrug in return. "Frank doesn't say much about it since it happened, but he was supposed to ride along with Deputy Dodds that night."

Mike looks to Chris questioningly. "What happened? Did Russling have anything to do with it?"

"Naw, he was out of town at some police convention. Frank said he passed-out just after he left here and missed the whole dang thing."

Mike lets the curious piece of information sink in, and then he waves as he turns to leave again. "Huh..."

Chris and Tom watch Mike step out the front entrance of the tavern. Tom heaves a sigh of relief, as he lifts his drink to his lips. "Jeez, those guys are really kind of depressing." The two friends exchange a bemused look and then Chris tips back a fresh beer and murmurs, "Cops and mechanics..."

Tom wonders aloud, "Yeah, what about 'em?"

"They both try to fix old shit."

Chapter 17

A lawn mower drones in the distance, while a police squad car sits in the shade of an overhanging oak tree. Inside the car, just off the main street, Mike sits and scribbles on a yellow pad of legal paper. There are several brief sentences of notes, but most of the markings are aimless and in random order. He glances over to the small hand-held voice recorder on the passenger side, next to him, and grabs it off the seat.

"Where are you, John...?"

Pressing the 'Play' button on the device, his own voice comes from the tiny speaker: *John Bratcher was headed out to the Connolly place that night after visiting with friends at Hall's Tap*. With a click, he presses 'Stop' and lowers the recorder to his lap, thinks a minute, and lifts it to press 'Play' once more: *Frank claims to have missed the ride-along with Deputy Dodds. Might have been the last one to speak to him...* Mike sits, lost in thought, as the recording trails on and the faraway sound of the lawn mower draws nearer.

"What am I missing?"

Unexpectedly, the rumbling sound of the lawn tractor dramatically increases, interrupting Mike's train of thought. He presses 'Stop' on the voice recorder and looks up to see Sticky driving his green John Deere riding lawn tractor. The old man is travelling down the middle of the street, perched on the yellow padded seat, with a can of beer in his hand. Sticky glances over at the parked, black and white squad car, as the riding mower rumbles loudly down the empty street. He briefly eyes the police vehicle before looking down at his open beer can. He lifts it to his mouth and takes on last gulp. There is a clanking rattle on the pavement, after he tosses the can away before pushing the mower's throttle to 'high'.

Sticky sits forward and grips the steering wheel with both hands. The lawn tractor's large, rear wheels chirp and the front tires jerk off the ground a second. A cloud of black, exhaust belches from under the plastic hood as the riding mower lunges forward.

In the squad car, Mike sits, in shock, as he observes Sticky hauling-ass down the middle of the street. He quickly tosses his pile of file notes and the voice recorder to the passenger seat and turns the key on the ignition. With lights flashing, the police car pulls out into the street and follows after the riding lawn mower in a low-speed chase.

In a matter of seconds, the police vehicle is right behind Sticky and the fleeing lawn tractor. After following for a block, Mike blips the police siren and gets on the loud speaker. "Sticky, pull that thing over to the side of the street!"

Sticky glances over his shoulder, squints past the flashing lights and through the windshield of the squad car. He puts on a guiltless smile, as he pulls back the throttle lever and turns off the engine key. Easing the mower to the right, Sticky glides to the curb. Mike follows along in the squad car and stops behind the halted lawn tractor.

As the deputy steps out of his vehicle, Sticky calls out, "Hey there, Deputy Mike! Sorry about the high-speed chase, but I thought you were Russling."

Mike approaches the riding mower and looks over the hot, ticking engine. "What the hell are you doing, Sticky?"

"Just heading home from work."

"You still have that part-time job keeping the school grounds?"

Sticky points at his official name badge sewn onto his shirt and nods his head. "Yeppers!"

"What happened to your truck?"

The old man slumps in the seat and shrugs faultless. "They won't let me drive it."

"Why not?"

"I don't know. Probably 'cause that asshole, Russling, took my license away. They're funny like that."

Mike shakes his head and can't help but be amused. "You lost your driver's license again?"

Sitting up proud and straight on the lawn tractor seat, Sticky puffs his chest out. "No sir, I didn't lose it, they took it!" He grins amiably and winks at Mike.

"Yeah, they stole it away for good this time. Don't mind though, since riding this bad boy keeps me in town and allows me time for other things."

Mike nods understandingly and curiously inquires, "What other things would those be?"

"Recreational activities such as drinking."

Appearing less pleased, Mike puts his foot on the mower deck of the lawn tractor. "Uh, that reminds me of that other thing." The deputy puts a hand to his knee and warns the driver. "You can't be drinking a beer while driving that thing down the middle of the street."

"I don't need a license to run it."

"Keep it on the grass."

Sticky frowns and appears somewhat concerned. "Hell, I could hit a tree or something and get hurt bad."

Mike shrugs apathetically and returns to the car with its bar of lights still flashing. He calls back over his shoulder, "Don't drink so much then."

After turning the ignition on the lawn mower, the engine starts up and Sticky revs the throttle. The tractor hood shakes and kicks out puffing clouds of thick, black smoke. "Give my regards to Russling."

Mike stops at the driver's side of the car and looks over the open door. "I mean it, Sticky. If you're drinking, keep it off the street." The old man on the tractor gives a friendly wave, pops the clutch and steers the rumbling mower to the grassy area along the road.

Chapter 18

The last rays of evening sunlight linger on the unoccupied brick buildings that form the town-center of Burlingview. Mike drives down the main street and, at the end of the road, turns in the direction of the police headquarters. He parks his squad across the street from the sheriff's car, switches off his headlights and watches the movement inside the station.

An outline of a shadow is seen against the closed blinds inside the sheriff's inner office as Mike murmurs to himself, "Working late again, Russling?" The sheriff's silhouette passes in front of the window and moves to where the cabinets line the wall. He disappears from sight and then appears again.

From the street outside, Mike sees the sheriff step out from the inner office. He moves to Mike's desk and shuffles through the papers on top. The sheriff pulls back Mike's chair, sits behind the desk and carefully goes through the drawers. As Mike witnesses the assault to his privacy, he mutters, "What the hell are you looking for now?" He looks over to the stack of files on the seat and then back out to the lit windows of the police station. "Damned if I'll let you get away with whatever you're up to." Without turning on his headlights, he quietly puts the car into gear and eases down the street.

~*~

A squad car sits at the end of the driveway leading to Mrs. Connolly's house-trailer. A television set inside the trailer casts a bright, blue light on the front bay windows. Slowly, a booted foot pushes down on the gas pedal and the police car rolls forward.

Staring with a glazed-over look in her clear-blue eyes, Mrs. Connolly sits on the couch, drink in hand, watching the television. Several more cocktail glasses, empty from days prior, sit before her on the coffee table. The creaking groan of the outer screen door is heard, and the trailer's front door begins to open. Perturbed, Mrs. Connolly glances over, obviously more than a bit intoxicated. "Russling, ya shit-heel! You missed dinner, and you'll have to warm it up yourself."

The door swings open wider to reveal Mike entering the room, looking around. "It's me, Mother."

Mrs. Connolly sits upright and swirls her mixed drink. "Oh, you missed dinner too." She takes a long sipping swallow and lays her head back on the cushion.

"I'm sorry... I forgot until a bit ago." Mike walks over, takes the empty glasses from the coffee table and puts them in the kitchen.   Turning her head toward him, she mumbles, "You hungry?"

"I'm okay."

Cicada

"Suit yerself..." He comes from the kitchen, sits in the chair next to his mother and looks to the drink in her hand. Defensively, she takes a long sip and looks up at her son. "Don't you look at me like that. I only have a few to relax." She takes another hefty sip of the drink and sets the glass tumbler down on the table.

Mike leans in and whispers, "You remember what we talked about yesterday?"

Mrs. Connolly rolls her eyes and takes a deep breath. "Oh God, leave it alone." She reaches out for her cocktail glass on the coffee table, but Mike grabs it first.

"You've had enough."

With obvious resentment, she glares at him with hollow eyes and grumbles, "Michael, now don't you be an asshole."

Mike sets the drink on the coffee table, out of her reach. He takes the television remote from the loveseat and turns down the TV's volume before scooting to the edge of his seat and looking directly at his mother. "John was headed out here that night he disappeared."

"So?"

"You saw him that night, is that right?"

"Who cares?"

"I do, Mother."

Mrs. Connolly attempts to reach past her son to get her drink, and Mike stops her by grabbing her extended arm. Taking the tone of an official police interrogator, he continues, "How long was he here?"

She shakes off his holding grip and pulls her arm away. "I don't remember."

"Mother, this is very important. I have to put this all together."

Mrs. Connolly sits back on the loveseat and her eyes moisten with painful memories. "Can't you just let it alone? The poor kid is long dead."

Mike stares at her a long while, trying to discover some missing part of the puzzle. "He's not dead, and I'm going to find out what happened."

A tear rolls down Mrs. Connolly's cheek and she turns her head to fix an empty glare on her son. "Why, Michael…?" Her eyes turn to her drink across the table, then back to Mike. "You need to make use of that big-city, police training that you abandoned me for?"

Mike appears emotionally hurt, and then he responds, "I never abandoned you."

His mother gives a sarcastic laugh and rolls her head back along the top of the loveseat. "If you hadn't skipped town and left me, just like your father did, I sure wouldn't be married to that asshole."

"I'm sorry…" Mike watches as his mother's eyes continue to cloud over in drunkenness. He leans closer and takes hold of her hands. "Mother, I really need to know this. What actually happened that night?"

Mrs. Connolly looks at Mike, and her hazy mind clears for just a moment. "I was drinking some. He stopped awhile, and then left. I don't remember anything else."

"Please… Try." Mike holds both his mother's hands firmly in his own, until she pulls them away. He sits back, frustrated, as she avoids eye contact with him while he continues his questioning. "I need to know everything that happened that night. Where does Hank Simms figure in this?"

The glowing television set flickers in the background, shimmering off her glistening-wet eyes. Taking a breath, she quietly responds, "He doesn't."

"What do you mean?"

Mrs. Connolly sits up and puts out her empty hand for her drink to be returned. Mike looks at her a long while, then gives back the cocktail. She takes a gulping swallow and delicately clears her throat. "I know what the reports say. Simms never assaulted me."

"But who was it?"

"Nobody did."

"Are you sure?"

Mrs. Connolly gives Mike a disgusted look. "Yes, I'm sure. Now, leave me alone."

Mike stares, perplexed. "I don't understand?"

Mrs. Connolly takes another big swallow and stares at the quiet flicker on the muted television. "Go away Michael… Leave me alone." After sitting in silence, Mike finally nods his head and gets up. Before slowly opening the door and exiting, he looks back to see his mother take yet another hefty gulp from her drink.

~*~

The squad car drives down a dark country road. Inside, the dim lights from the dashboard illuminate heavy lines of concentration creased on Mike's features. He suddenly slams on the brakes and pulls the car to the side of the road. Grabbing his voice recorder, he hits 'Record'.

Eric H. Heisner

Mike sits in silence until he pushes 'Stop' on the device. He lowers the small, battery-operated recorder to his lap and rolls down the window to let in some fresh air. The loud chattering sound of cicadas nearly overwhelms him, as he sits alone in the darkness at the side of the empty road.

Chapter 19

The neon sign of "Frank's Engine & Transmission Repair" casts a bright light over the entrance of the service garage. Mike's police car is parked across the street, discreetly hidden in the shadows. He sits in the car and watches as a section of the glowing sign occasionally blinks off and on.

Placed on his lap are the note pad and voice recorder. Holding something metallic in his left hand, Mike gently rubs the texture absentmindedly between his thumb and fingers. He pushes his hair back on his forehead and looks down to the hand holding the star-shape of his father's sheriff's badge.

In the dim light, Mike stares at his notes and rests his finger on the drifter's name, *Hank Simms*. The name is circled several times with relevant information from the police file scribbled in the margin: *Apprehended inside transmission repair garage at 05:00 hours.* Mike looks up at the garage then looks back down to the small cluster of police files on the passenger seat. He draws one out, spreads it open across the middle of the seat and reads: *Suspect sustained three gunshot wounds before being subdued... declared dead at 05:17 hours.*

Mike stares at the file information, glances up at the repair shop again and then looks forward through the windshield. He closes his eyes slightly and murmurs aloud, "Shot three times? Why would he come back to town after killing the deputy?"

Mike looks again to the garage now owned by Frank. He studies the design of the building from roof to sidewalk. Letting his gaze skim over the details again, his eyes pause on a small painted-over window near the peak of the roof gable. Mike looks back down at his notes, writes something along the margin and returns his gaze to the garage's attic window. He takes a deep breath and sighs, "What did you see?"

~*~

In a working class neighborhood, a quaint, one-story, ranch-style home has a police car parked in its driveway. Sunrise brightens the brick home, but heavy drapes pulled across its front windows block the morning light.

In one of the bedrooms, the orange glow of daylight peeks through the edge of the window covering. Mike lies, gently snoring, face down on the bed. The stillness is broken when the rotary phone on the bedside table rings sharply, jolting Mike from his slumber. Jutting his arm out from under the covers, he reaches for the telephone receiver and yanks it from the cradle. "Hello...?" Still face down on the pillow, Mike remains motionless as the female voice on the other end of the line chatters excitedly. Suddenly, he tosses off the crumpled blankets and sits up, alert. "He used a shotgun? Anyone hurt?" Mike listens a moment and sweeps his hand over his sleepy eyes, replying, "Alright, I will be right over." He hangs up the phone, slides off the mattress and quickly goes to the bedroom closet to put on his police uniform.

~*~

A police car races down the quiet street, lights flashing, and swings into the driveway of a house at the edge of town. Tires screech to a halt, the driver's-side door swings open and Mike leaps from the car, pistol drawn. Hunkered down low, he moves around the front bumper of the idling squad car and then rushes toward the front entry of the house. With his back against the wall, he reaches over and hammers his fist on the aluminum screen door, rattling it in its frame. "Anyone there? Come out slowly!" The lace curtains covering the front picture-window peel back slightly, and a man with wispy, white hair peeks out. From beside the door, Mike looks over to peer through the wide window to the old man. "Come out, Mister Thompson."

There is a rustle of movement inside the dark home, and the sound of the deadbolt on the front door sliding free. The interior door slowly opens a crack, and Mister Thompson appears behind the screen-door with an antique, double-barreled shotgun slung across his arm. Eyes wide at the sight of the firearm, Mike braces himself and stands at the ready, both hands firm on his pistol. "Put the shotgun down!"

Mister Thompson draws back in and hollers at Mike. "You put your gun down!"

The police deputy reaches his hand to the screen-door handle to pull it open but finds it latched. He stands aside and repeats himself, this time, more officiously. "This is the Police. Put the gun down and open this door."

The old man defensively draws back inside further, closing the door a bit more. "I'm not opening up until you put your gun away, Michael."

"Open it!"

"Hell no!"

Frustrated with the impasse, Mike lowers the tone of his voice and adds sternly. "I need you to open the door."

"Not gonna happen."

"Why not?

"Are you going to shoot me?"

"No."

The door opens a bit wider, and the old man peeks out. "Then put your gun away, kiddo."

"Goddammit..." Aggravated, Mike heaves a deep breath and holsters his gun. Mister Thompson peeks out from the interior and sets the shotgun to the side of the entryway. He reaches outside to unlock the screen door, and Mike puts his hand to the handle trigger, clicks it and swings it open. "Come on out here."

The old man hesitantly steps out of the house, stands on the front porch and looks at the police lights, still flashing. "You gonna shut those lights off?"

Cicada

Not wanting to get into another battle of wills, Mike stares at Mister Thompson. Then he nods his head slightly, walks over to the police car, steps around the open door and switches off the light bar. Gazing at the old man through the windshield, Mike reaches over the steering column and turns off the ignition key. The deputy stands beside the vehicle, looks down the quiet street and swings the car door closed. Weary, Mike heaves a sigh and patiently walks back to the front porch of the house to where Mister Thompson waits. "Sir… Is that your shotgun inside?"

The old man nods his head and leans his hand on the doorframe. "Yep, it is."

"You going to give it to me?"

"Nope, sure ain't. Been in the family a long time."

Mike notices Mister Thompson glance inside and assumes the shotgun is leaned on the wall, just by the door. He stands on the lower step and looks up at the old man. "You know the rules in town. I can't let you keep shooting at anything that bothers you."

"I didn't shoot at you, did I?"

Mike nods his agreement and takes a measured breath. "I got called over here because you were reported to be shooting a firearm off your back porch this morning."

"Damned nosey neighbors…"

"You can't be shooting a shotgun off in town and think people won't notice."

"When I moved here, this wasn't *in* town."

Mike nods understandingly and looks down the street and its few houses. "What were you shooting at?"

"Varmints."

The deputy drops his gaze at the hopeless situation. "Does the neighbor's dog fall into that category?"

"Yep."

"You can't do that. That's not how things work in a civilized community."

Mister Thompson moves his foot to keep open the aluminum screen door as a gentle breeze blows it closed. "Hey kiddo, you mess with me or mine, and you're damn sure I'm gonna come a' shootin'."

With his foot on the first stair, Mike climbs another step and the old man moves further inside the open doorway. Mike puts up both hands to stop him, speaking calmly. "Mister Thompson, you will have to give me that shotgun, or you need to promise me never to shoot it off in town again."

"Are those the orders from Russling?"

"Why?"

"I just wanted to know if what you say has any teeth to back it up, or just bark."

Mike stares up at the older man quizzically and replies, "I am an officer of the law in this town."

"Dependin' on where you stand with the sheriff, somethin' like that doesn't always mean much."

"What do you mean by that?"

"The same as always was, around here. Either you're his toady, or you won't last long."

Mike gets somewhat heated under the collar with hurt pride, and embarrassment, as he confronts the older man. "Well, I'm not his... you know what."

Cicada

Mister Thompson looks the youthful deputy over and gives an acknowledging sigh. "Well then, Mikey, you might jest want to go on 'n git then. Head back to the big city where you can really be somethin'." Mister Thompson steps out past the door again and grunts. "Ain't you noticed, this has-been town is wrapped up in Russling's sick little package. It's best to leave it alone, if you don't want to get twisted up with it."

Mike shakes his head, and moves to his car. "Please, Mister Thompson. No more shooting in town."

The old man standing at the darkened doorway nods. He calls out as the deputy approaches the side of the squad car. "Hey, is Frank in any kind of trouble?"

Mike stops and turns to the old man. "Why do you say that? Did he mention something?"

"No… Just saw you outside his shop last night."

Mike looks inside the car to the notebook and files on the seat. He looks up to Mister Thompson again. "Does anyone live above the shop anymore?"

"Not since he bought the place, over a dozen years ago. He lived there awhile, but no one else since."

Mike nods thinking. "Who lived there before?"

"No one regular that I know of, ever. I think they lent it out to different fellas that worked temporary in the shop."

Mike turns back to Mister Thompson on the porch. "Don't remember anyone specific?"

"Kid, no one stays long in this town. Either you're sucked in for good, or you're encouraged to leave in a hurry. Your Sheriff Russling sees to that."

"Yeah, you mentioned that."

Opening the car door, Mike is about to get in when Mister Thompson calls out again. "So, Frank is not in trouble or anything?"

Mike swings the door open wider, puts one foot into the car and peers over the windshield at Mr. Thompson. "No. Your son is clear of the law."

Chapter 20

The main street businesses are just beginning to open up as the town café fills with customers. An old truck rumbles down the street and turns in front of the transmission repair garage. The pickup truck stops, the engine turns off and Frank steps out to see a parked squad car positioned across the street. Letting the truck door hang open, Frank walks the short distance and approaches the stationary police vehicle.

Frank peers through the steamed-up car windows to see Mike sleeping uncomfortably, upright in the driver's seat. He leans in closer, about to rap his knuckles on the glass window, when Mike's eyes open to look straight at Frank. Both men startle, and Frank jumps back to trip on his heels, stumbles to the middle of the street, exclaiming, "Shit-damn"

As the window rolls down, Mike tosses his notepad to the passenger side seat and looks at Frank. "Good morning?"

"What the hell are you doing here?"

"I need to talk with you, Frank."

Standing out in the middle of the empty street, Frank looks around and then spins away to walk back to the garage. "I told you. I've got nothing to say to you."

Mike pushes the squad car door open and follows. "C'mon Frank, we were good friends all through school."

Frank gets to the shop door, takes out his keys and unlocks it. "Just go away, and leave me alone."

"I can't do that. John needs our help."

The shop entrance door swings open, and Frank turns to Mike. He shakes his head mournfully. "Give it a rest. You're a few decades too late. The guy is dead."

Frank enters the repair shop and flips on the lights while Mike remains in the entry. The lines of fluorescent bulbs hum and gradually flicker on. "How do you know for sure? Did you see something?"

Frank pivots to the town deputy and is about to say something, but holds back instead. He studies Mike and tries to sense what he might actually know. The two stare at each other as the bright daylight shines in through the shopfront windows, mixing with the artificial light inside the garage. Frank finally shakes his head, looks away and goes to a clutter of parts on a workbench. "He's dead. Leave it alone."

Mike takes a step inside while tightening the tuck on his uniform shirt. "How is Hank Simms involved in all this? Frank shakes his head and lifts a carburetor part to examine it under the workbench light. Mike stares intently at Frank. "How well did you know Simms?"

Cicada

While trying to ignore Mike's questioning, the mechanic glances over at the deputy, sets down the part and grabs a pipe wrench. Mike continues, "I know that you worked with him here at the shop."

Frank drops the wrench and, over his shoulder, barks, "Then, what the hell are you bothering me for?"

"I need you to help me fill in some of the blanks."

Placing both his hands on the edge of the workbench, Frank heaves a breath of air and lowers his chin to his chest. Realizing that Mike won't leave it alone without something, he sighs and responds, "He rolled into town the week after I started here full time."

"Did you talk about anything?"

Frank turns to face Mike again. He leans on the workbench and folds his arms. "No, we didn't have any long conversations. He got locked up a few days after he got here for public intoxication."

"Did he know my mother?"

Troubled, Frank's intense gaze lowers to the floor. "How should I know?" He looks up at Mike. "She came by here sometimes trying to sell one of those cars your dad had."

At the mention of his absent father, Mike feels a cold chill run down his spine but does his best to hide his feelings. He pauses before he responds. "She must have talked to him."

"Maybe she did or not. Who the hell cares?" Frank grabs a dirty rag and wraps it around his clenched fist. He leans back on the jumbled workbench and stares at Mike. "Did that fill in any of the blanks for you?" Frank squints. "What are you really trying to find out?"

"I just want to know what happened that night, and why our friend John disappeared."

The bright, morning sunlight streams in from the shop doorway, while Frank stares ominously at his high school classmate and snorts. "You mean to try and find out what happened to your father... Or who assaulted your mother?" Mike's features immediately flush with a mix of anger and humiliation, as he feebly utters, "She says she wasn't raped."

With a deliberate breath, Frank looks away and mutters, "Yeah, she usually just gave it away."

Mike shakes off his awkwardness and glares. "What are you implying by that?"

Immediately regretting what was said, Frank shrugs. "She was lonely a lot, I hear."

"She says she wasn't assaulted."

Frank straightens up and glares at his former friend. "Then what the hell is this all about?"

His mind reeling, trying to get the sequence of events in his head and to suppress the swelling of confused emotions, Mike blurts out, "The sheriff is covering up something, and I want to nail him for it." He looks into the eyes of his friend and states firmly, "Who shot Deputy Dodds, who involved my mother in this, and what happened to our friend John?"

It is uncomfortably quiet as Frank slowly makes his way toward Mike. "I'll tell you who it wasn't." Nervously, Frank glances over his shoulder to the stairway leading up to the loft apartment at the rear of the shop. He moves closer. "Hank Simms didn't kill a deputy or rape anyone that night. He might have been a

Cicada

hopeless drunk, though, and that's what eventually got him murdered."

Taken aback by this new evidence, Mike wants more. "How do you know this?"

Frank steps even closer to get right into Mike's face. "He was still locked up that Friday night when it happened." Frank glances past Mike's shoulder to the bright light coming in through the open doorway. He hesitates, then finishes. "That was until our own Sheriff Russling fixed up the police report and brought him here to the garage and murdered him. It sure wrapped up the case nicely though didn't it?"

Mike stands in a state of shock. The hairs on the nape of his neck prickle as he softly inquires, "He *brought* him here? Why here?"

The mechanic dourly replies, "The bastard didn't even take the handcuffs off until after he shot him the third time."

"You saw that?"

Disgusted, Frank exhales blatantly through his nose. "You got answers to some of your questions now. I bet you can't do a damn thing with it that will make any difference." He turns from Mike and waves his arm, shooing him away. "Get the hell out of here." Mike stands silhouetted in the entry, with the blinding sunlight of a new day streaming in. Frank walks toward the dim unlit area at the back of the shop. "Go away, and leave it alone."

Chapter 21

The sound of a coffee machine gurgling out a fresh pot of brew is interrupted by the scraping sound of the front door on the entry mat. Mike enters the police station looking as if he had slept in his squad car all night. He walks past Mary, sitting at the front desk, and she looks up at him with a smile. "Good morning, Mike."

"Yeah… Morning."

"Did you take care of Mister Thompson?"

He pauses on his way through the office to look at her. "I handled it." Mary puts on an expression of blamelessness and then avoids the irritated deputy by returning to her task. Mike continues to his desk and looks around purposefully. "Anything going on today?"

"There's a game over at the field at one o'clock."

Not finding what he was looking for at his workspace, Mike returns across the office to the receptionist desk in front. He leans on the wall, running his hand through his mussed hair, as he looks to a baseball on Mary's desk. "You going?"

She gives a dramatic huff. "Well, if I could ever get all my work done, I could actually have a life outside this office."

Mike rubs his tired eyes and looks down at the piles of organized papers on her desktop. She grins at him playfully. "Yes, I'm leaving here at noon to watch." Mike forces a smile, and Mary twirls a pen, looking him over. "You look tired, Mike. Are you okay?"

With a mild shrug, Mike jiggles the ring of keys in his front pocket. "I'm going to head home and get some sleep. Call me if you need me." He walks to the entrance doors and slowly pulls one open. Looking away from the morning light, he glances over his shoulder to Mary. "Is Russling around?"

She clicks her pen a few times and taps her desktop. "He's out there somewhere." Mike nods as he exits the station.

~*~

The town park is a scattering of shade trees with a kids' playground and a baseball diamond on a patch of short grass. A rusted, wire-mesh backstop is flanked by a set of old wooden bleacher seats on both sides. The ballgame is just about to get underway with players beginning to warm up, playing catch while a crowd gathers at the sidelines.

Driving the police vehicle into the park's gravel lot, Mike looks out at the dedicated memorial sign that reads: *Harvey Lust Field, est. 1959.* From across the wide parking lot, Mike can see the ball game starting, and that

Cicada

there are about two dozen people in the stands. He parks the police car in the grass at the edge of the lot, pointed toward town with an easy access out. Despite the unlikelihood of any sort of emergency, his police training and years in the city keep him vigilant.

The umpires call out the start of the game as Mike approaches the field. Dressed in his police uniform, the new deputy instinctively scans the sea of recognizable faces in the bleachers. He notices that several townspeople react to his presence and purposefully avoid eye contact with him.

Through the metal-mesh backstop, he spots Aunt Missy cooking hamburgers and hotdogs at her handy kitchen setup. Looking around, he walks past the first group of bleachers and, three benches up, spots Mary reading. She peers up from the book on her lap and smiles at the deputy, as he stops and stands beside her. While watching the field, Mike greets her. "Hello."

"You look a bit more chipper. Feeling better?"

"Much better, thanks. Who's gonna win?"

Mary scans the ball field, assessing the players as they take their regular positions, and then smiles aside to Mike. "Frank's team will win by two."

Mike leans his arm on the seat next to her and grunts. "With your mind for projection of events, you should have been a bookie."

"No fun in it, since I'm always right."

Mike scans the baseball diamond, noticing custom t-shirts with *Frank's Transmission Repair* against *Bratcher's Hardware*. He also sees that Frank isn't dressed to play and is instead, standing on the team sidelines.

"Doesn't Frank usually play?" Turning a page, without looking from her book, Mary replies, "Yeah, but he said he's been feeling out of sorts."

Mike glances at Mary, still staring at the book in her lap. She reads and, only occasionally, looks up at the game. Mike nods at the book. "How do you always know everything that goes on while you sit there reading that book?"

Mary looks at Mike and then past him, over his shoulder. "I have ears, too." She goes back to her book, whispering, "Russling just got here."

Mike looks around the park and notices the sheriff approaching the baseball field from the parking lot. "Mary? Did you hear him coming?"

A mischievous smile crosses Mary's lips, and she winks at Mike before watching the ballgame for a moment. "No... You can always tell that easily by watching the crowd." Mike's quick scan of the bleachers brings a sinking feeling, as he notices a similar reaction to when he approached the field.

Mike observes as faces turn away and smiles become cautious with elusive side-glances. "Damn... Does everyone feel like that when I come around, too?"

"Depends..."

They are interrupted when Mr. Bratcher slides along the bench seat just below Mary and reaches out to give Mike a friendly nudge. "Hey there! Whose team you on?"

Mike looks at the affable hardware man and smiles. "I'm just an observer. I don't have any money on the game."

Cicada

The older man smiles in return. "That's good 'cause Frank's team whips the snot out of us every time."

Mike seems at ease, until Mr. Bratcher reaches into his pocket and pulls a pair of freshly made keys. He holds the set out to Mike. "Here. You left these at the store the other day. Thought you'd be missing them."

Mike tentatively puts his hand out, and Mr. Bratcher drops them into his open palm. "How much do I owe you?"

Mr. Bratcher slides off the bleacher benches and stands next to the deputy. "Throw in a few extra cheers for our side, and we'll call it even." Mike tenses up as the hardware man pats him on the shoulder, leans over and lowers his voice. "Better get back over to my team, or they'll figure I folded."

He looks at his friend's father and nods. "Thanks."

Mike watches as Mr. Bratcher travels to the opposite set of bleachers, clapping and cheering his team on as he goes. Mary extends her hand and clears her throat. "Someday, I was going to ask you about those."

He hands the set of keys over to her. "Sorry."

Mary tucks the keys away in her purse, as Mike scans the cheering crowd of spectators. He sees Russling talking with Aunt Missy, as she cooks on the grill. Sticky steps up to buy a hotdog, and he turns his back on the sheriff to make a comical face to anyone watching.

Turning his attention back to the baseball game, Mike notices Frank subtly observing him. He waves to his old school friend, and Frank turns away, pretending not to notice. Glancing toward Missy again, Mike sees that Russling is gone. He scans the crowd and Mary watches him as he looks the field over searching for the sheriff. Finally, he stops his hunt when Aunt Missy starts waving him over to the outdoor grill. "You hungry?"

"No thanks."

Mike gazes at Mary while she looks at her book. "I'll see you later."

She traces her finger under a sentence on the page, as if she had been reading without interruption, and nods. "Okay, see you at the office." Mike watches until she turns the page, and then he moves around the caged backstop toward the burger stand.

~*~

Coming up alongside the serving table, Mike tries to keep out of everyone's way, as Aunt Missy talks incessantly to her customers while hustling grub. There is a brief pause in sales, and Missy casts a knowing look over to the deputy. "Hey there, sweetie. Who were you looking for over there?"

Mike shrugs without answering, expecting Missy to let it go and continue on with her business. He stares out to the field, until he senses her scrutiny as she waits for an answer. Feeling put on the spot, he fumbles out a reticent response, "Uh, just looking to see who's out here today."

"Just about everyone in town is here. You want to get a good pulse for the community, this is where you feel for it."

Mike glances around at the mostly recognizable faces. "I haven't been around here in a long time."

Cicada

"Well, welcome back. Take it easy, sugar... I'm not the only one who notices you looking." Aunt Missy gives a knowledgeable wink and hurries over to check the grill.

Suddenly feeling uncomfortable and out of place in his police uniform, Mike turns to the neighboring crowd of faces and begins to get a strong sense of paranoia. Everyone seems to be whispering or gesturing and nodding in his direction. The rumbling murmur of the town crowd becomes deafening, as he imagines he hears his name among the unintelligible gossip.

Aunt Missy breaks him from his daydream, patting him on the cheek as she shoves a loaded burger basket at him. "This'll put some meat on them bones. Now go on, and don't you be an agitator." Mike forces a smile at Aunt Missy, and, as she hustles back to her restaurant business, the loud crack of a bat connecting to a baseball puts the crowd on its feet.

Chapter 22

The early morning sun shines through the doors of the police station. At the front entrance, Mike puts his key in the lock and is startled to see Mary already seated her desk, working. She looks up from her papers, smiling a greeting as he enters. "Good morning, Mike."

"Hello. What are you doing here on a Sunday?"

She watches the door swing shut. "The same reason you are… I have nothing else to do."

Mike goes to his desk and finds everything seemingly in place where he left it. He glances over to the sheriff's office, with its lights off and the door closed. Moving around to the side of his desk, he calls over toward the front of the station. "Mary, did Russling say what time he's coming in?"

"Sunday, he usually comes in around ten."

After noticing that the clock on the wall reads seven-forty, he glances again to the office door, then to the entry. Mike moves to the sheriff's office, out of

Mary's line of sight. He grips the door handle, gently gives the knob a twist and is surprised to find it locked. Mike is about to call out to Mary when a ringing telephone interrupts him.

Mary answers the phone call at the front desk. In a state of alarm, she responds to the caller, "Oh my goodness! Okay, I'll send him right over."

Mike rushes to the front of the station and stands before her questioning, "What is it? What happened?"

Mary takes a breath and, with a sad expression, hangs up the telephone, looks across her desk to Mike and replies. "It's about Sticky…"

"Yeah?"

"He's on that tractor-mower, over at Second Street and Fowler, doing circles in the intersection."

A flush of anger swells, as Mike shakes his head and digs his keys from his pocket. "Dammit, Sticky…!" Irritated by the disregard to his warning, he grumbles, "Is he drunk? I told him to keep it off the street."

Mary stands up behind her desk, mouth agape, as Mike rushes from the station and climbs into the police car parked out front.

~*~

A zooming car engine is heard speeding down the main street, as Mike drives the few short blocks through town. Just a street over, Sticky and his lawn-tractor are circling in the crosswalks. A few cars wait nearby, watching. The police car's lights flash on and Mike blips the siren. He slowly drives into the blocked intersection, getting as close as he can to the circling path

Cicada

of the lawn-tractor. The deputy steps out of his squad car, and stands frozen behind the open door.

Emergency lights flashing, the patrol car sits idle as the tractor passes by. A saddened sense of loss sweeps over Mike, as he gets a better look at Sticky slumped over the mower's steering wheel. Slowly, Mike steps away from the police car and approaches the mower.

Choking back strong emotions, Mike watches as Sticky, his lap partly soaked by a spilt can of beer, takes his last ride. As the wandering lawn-tractor passes again, Mike jumps to the side step on the mower deck and grabs the steering wheel. He reaches over to ease the throttle downward and steers the mower toward his parked squad car.

When Mike kills the engine, the tractor rolls to a stop and the beer can from Sticky's lap tumbles to the pavement with a hollow clank. Mike steps off the mower deck, and the hot, ticking motor gives off waves of heat. Performing his duty, the deputy directs the waiting cars through the cleared intersection and then steps around the open door to sit in his patrol car.

Mike grabs the microphone from the clip on the dashboard radio as he looks through the windshield to Sticky, still slumped over the tractor steering wheel. His chin quivers, as he swallows and clicks on the handheld receiver. "Hello… This is Officer Connolly."

There is a steady stream of static until Mary's soft voice breaks in. "Go ahead, Mike."

"Mary, could you call an ambulance over here?"

"Is he okay?"

Eric H. Heisner

Mike looks out at Sticky one more time and exhales, "No, he's not. Could you please inform the morgue as well?" Slouching down on the driver's seat, Mike lowers the radio receiver to his lap and lays his head back on the headrest. Tears form at the corners of his eyes and steadily roll down his cheeks.

Chapter 23

Mike forcefully pushes through the police station doors, looks around momentarily and strides toward his own desk. Mary gazes up at Mike as he passes by her and quietly utters, "I'm sorry about your Uncle."

Appearing to be on a mission, Mike tosses his keys into the lone tray on his desk and heads to the sheriff's office door. Again, he finds it locked. "Mary, come here. Bring your keys."

From the front reception area, Mary eases around the corner and looks at Mike. "I don't think I should."

He motions to the locked door. "Open it, please."

Mary obediently moves to the sheriff's private office with her ring of keys, holds the door handle and unlocks it. She nervously asks, "Are you okay? You don't look too well."

He gently moves her aside and enters the office. "Thank you. You may go back to your desk now." Hesitantly, Mary backs away as Mike disappears inside.

Mike heads straight to the sheriff's desk, grabs a set of keys from the center drawer and moves to the line of cabinets. He opens the metal drawer and reaches for the file on John. Thumbing through the scant remaining pages, he realizes that the majority of the official reports are missing.

A flutter of panic sweeps over him, and he murmurs, "No, he couldn't have..." Mike flips through the pages again, shaking his head in disbelief. "He took most of it out?!?"

Behind, a booming voice sends ice through his veins. "That's right, Michael."

The deputy spins around to see the sheriff standing in the office doorway. Sheriff Russling stands in partial shadow, but his eyes reflect a glint of contempt. "I know what you're up to, ya little shit-bird. You never did like me very much." He shifts his weight and leans a shoulder on the door frame. "I'll be damned if I'm going to let you think you've got something on me."

Guilty of being caught with his hand in the cookie jar, Mike gathers his wits and replies. "I know you killed him."

Russling snorts and lets out a small chuckle. "Who?"

The sheriff moves into the private office, steps around his desk and takes a seat. Leather squeaks, as he pushes back in his padded chair.

Mike looks at the file and sets the incomplete folder back in the open drawer. "You know who I'm talking about."

Cicada

Flashing a wolfish grin, Russling responds smugly, "Actually, I don't."

"You killed him in cold blood and you will answer for it."

Sheriff Russling leans forward in the creaking chair and puts both of his elbows on top of his desk with a solid thud. With deliberate malevolence, he stares at the new deputy. "You don't know what the hell you're talking about, do you? Where did you come up with all this half-assed information?" He thinks a moment and adds, "I hope it wasn't one of your old buddies that put this fanciful notion in your head."

The hollowness at the pit of his stomach begins to twist, as Mike realizes he has put his friend in a dangerous position. "No one has forgotten what really happened. You'll be held accountable, when the truth comes out."

The sheriff tilts his head and sits back in the chair. "Which truth are you speaking of? I doubt anyone cares about pursuing an incident that happened such a long time ago." The sheriff puts his hands to the chair's padded armrests and rocks back. "Most everyone has let it slip their minds. You would be wise to do the same."

"Not everyone has forgotten."

"Mike, you want to be a fine police officer, like your daddy was?" The sheriff smirks. "Remember, I'm the sheriff, and you're the deputy. What I say goes, in this here town. That's the way your daddy ran it in his day, and that's the way I run it now."

The mention of his father troubles Mike emotionally. "You're nothing like my dad."

Eric H. Heisner

Russling sits back in his leather throne and rocks it. "Who do you think trained me?" He stops the padded chair from creaking, sits up and stares across the room to Mike. "Now… I'd appreciate it if you would put those files back, lock the drawer like you found it and return my keys."

Resentful, Mike stuffs the remainder of the file papers back in the folders and slides the drawer closed. He turns the lock and removes the key from the cabinet.

Still seated, Russling reaches out and taps his finger at the middle of his desk. Mike walks over and places the keys before the sheriff and asks, "Where did you put the rest of the pages from the report?"

Russling grins and glances to the open door. He raises his voice and calls out to the receptionist. "Mary, could you come in here a moment?"

The two wait, until Mary appears at the door.

"Yes, sir?"

"Mary, could you please empty my shredder bin. Somehow it seems to be all full again." She keeps her gaze lowered and leans down to remove the paper-filled bag from the shredding machine.

Russling smiles priggishly, as Mike stands before the desk, dumbfounded. He watches Mary, as she takes out another plastic bag and fits it under the shredder. Holding the stuffed bag of destroyed documents, she looks to the pair facing-off at the desk. "Anything else?"

The sheriff smiles satisfied and waves her off. "No, that will pretty much take care of it. Thank you."

Mike can hardly contain himself as Mary carries the bag of shredded paper from the room. "You can't…!"

Cicada

Russling interrupts his pathetic plea and rocks in his chair. "Go home and get some rest. You look beat."

"Damn you…"

"What's that?"

Flushed with anger, Mike glares at the sheriff. He tries to speak, but he can't find the words to express his rage. Russling waits for the deputy's response and lightly adds, "Did you get that shotgun away from old man Thompson?"

"I, uh… I took care of it."

Entertained, the sheriff shakes his head doubtfully. "Did you really?" He rocks his chair forward and puts his large forearms to the desk edge and clasps his hands together. His gaze lowers to the cabinet drawer keys, at the center of the desktop, then lifts up to Mike again. "Just you remember… People get hurt when they get into other people's business. Straighten out your priorities, and come back when you think you can handle your duties."

Russling stares at Mike, across the desk, as the deputy gets his resentment under control and nods. The sheriff tilts his head and puts a finger to the lower part of his ear. "What was that? I didn't quite hear." The sheriff stares coldly. "Did you say something?"

Choking down his pride, Mike utters, "Yes, sir."

The sheriff pats his palms together and nods smugly. "Good, glad to hear it. Now get out of my office, and shut the door behind you." Mike hesitates a moment, and Russling mockingly brushes his fingers at him in a shooing fashion. Feeling crushed, Mike leaves the sheriff's office, pulling the door shut behind him.

Chapter 24

Birds chirp in the trees, as Mike drives the squad car down an alleyway behind Main Street. He lets the car roll along on the gravel mixed with broken asphalt, until he hits the breaks and stops directly behind the hardware store. The police car idles, as it sits several yards from the rear loading-bay doors.

Mike studies the back side of the building, wearily staring at the double doors, half-expecting to see John again. He stares at the open padlock, hanging from the latch loop. The police car remains stopped in its tracks, while the engine softly idles in the vacant alleyway, with no one else around. Suddenly, Mike feels a slight surge of excitement, as someone appears at the loading dock bay.

As Mr. Bratcher steps over to a dolly, stacked high with boxes, and tips it back on its wheels, the sound of an engine in the alley catches his attention. He turns to see Mike in his car, gives a friendly wave and quietly watches the car drive off.

~*~

On the shoulder of the two-lane blacktop, beyond the edge of town, the squad car sits parked. Behind the wheel, note pad and files on his lap, Mike reads over the description of the incident in the abridged police report.

The car door swings open and Mike steps out with the statement page describing the encounter with Deputy Dodds. While he reads the incident report, he slowly plays through the series of tragic events. Stopping in the middle of the road as he reaches the end of the account, he notices a black oil stain that resembles a darkened pool of blood. He stares hypnotically at the stain, unable to look away.

Seemingly from out of nowhere, the rumble of an oncoming cattle truck is heard, quickly followed by the warning blare of an air-horn. Mike looks up to see a stake-bed truck coming, directly at him. He quickly jumps out of the vehicle's path, and the farm truck zooms past, leaving him in a cloud of clinging field dust.

Mike watches the truck slow to a groaning stop and then sits, waiting in the road. The back-up lights flicker on, followed by a sharp, pulsing warning beep and the whine of the transmission going in reverse, as the brake lights fade out. The cattle truck slowly backs down the road and stops behind the car on the shoulder.

Aged steel groans, as the driver's-side door pushes open. An older man in workman's attire peeks his head out and looks back at the deputy in the road. "Is that you, Mike?" The never-to-retire farmer, Eli Warren squints his eyes and sun-wrinkled features to study the officer standing by the police car. "By golly, it is!"

Cicada

"Hello, Mister Warren."

Eli climbs down from the truck cab and ambles bow-legged toward Mike. "Sorry 'bout that… But you were standing in the road so long, I didn't think you were gonna move to the side in time." The farmer dusts his pant-legs off and smiles. "Hell, if I would've mistaken you for Russling, you never would've heard a horn, that's fer sure."

Mike glances down at the file papers in his hand. "Yeah, it was my fault."

Eli looks around at the unpopulated rural landscape, just beyond the reach of the town. "What'cha doin' out here? Did your squad car break down?"

"I was thinking."

The old farmer rubs the whisker stubble on his chin. "Thinking, huh? There are much better places fer that sort of thing than the middle of the road. A feller could git killed."

"Sorry, Mister Warren. I'll watch out next time."

The old farmer gives the younger man a kindly smile as he glances up from the law badge on Mike's police uniform. "Since you're an adult and all now, ya can just call me Eli."

"Alright, Eli."

Mike walks to the squad car and tosses the file report pages in through the open driver's side window. Interested, Eli ambles over and watches the papers flutter to the seat. "What were you trying to figure out?" Mike leans on the car door and turns to Eli. "Nothing."

Cocking his head, the timeworn farmer squints at Mike before stating, "Something's eatin' at ya, 'n it looks to got a good hold on ya, too. What is it?"

Mike crosses his arms across his chest and half-heartedly considers relating his list of troubles to the farmer. "I don't know. I'm going crazy trying to think it all through."

With a bow-legged hobble, Eli moseys over and eases a thigh up onto the fender of the police vehicle. "Lay it on me."

Mike hangs his head down and heaves a reluctant sigh. "The whole thing all sounds crazy to me now. If it gets out, the entire town will think I'm nuts."

"Try me. Hell, everyone thinks I'm nuts already."

Mike ponders a short while and then decides to unload some of his mental burden on the farmer. "I can't believe it, but I saw John Bratcher alive the other day."

Curious, Eli looks at Mike and nods his head while the deputy continues his story. "I know what I thought I saw... He was talking to his father in the back of his folk's store."

Eli listens and doesn't seem to appear too alarmed. "What did he say to ya?"

Stunned by Eli's unruffled reaction and the obvious question, Mike utters, "He didn't say anything at all. I tried to catch him, but he disappeared."

Eli's eyes go wide. "Vanished?"

"Not vanished exactly... Just gone by the time I got to where he was." Studying Mike, the farmer remains silent and nods again, waiting for more. The deputy casts his gaze out away from his attentive

Cicada

audience to the long stretches of field. Mike continues, "He's alive and hiding, and I know it has something to do with Russling. I just can't prove anything."

Eli frowns. "Well, that don't sound that crazy."

Mike looks confused. "Really?"

"Career suicide maybe... But not crazy."

Mike nods his agreement. "Yeah, I know."

The old farmer wipes his hands on the front of his shirt, glances at his dirt-creased palms, and then looks at Mike. "John is alive. Don't know 'bout him hiding though. I'd say, just staying gone." The old farmer shrugs nonchalantly and Mike stares back, dumbfounded.

Chapter 25

A rural farmstead sits just a few miles away from town, surrounded by fields of crops and freshly-plowed land. Mike's squad car is parked behind Eli's dusty cattle truck, near a two-story brick house and several barn outbuildings. Several farm implements, sit randomly parked in the area, grass growing high around them.

The large, white barn is in desperate need of paint, and several windows are broken. Inside the old, wooden structure, Eli stands next to a tractor rebuild project with piles of engine parts strewn about. Looking for something, he digs through a tool box as he talks. "Like I said to ya before, nobody asked me after it happened. Besides, that dumb-asshole, Russling, knows better than to come 'round here asking questions."

"You don't get along with the sheriff?"

Eli stifles a laugh, as he finds the tool he's looking for. "You could call it that. He's been a lowlife, jack-off, panty-waist ever since that day I first met him in grammar school. You know, if it wasn't for that badge he hides behind, I'd wallop him every chance I got."

Dismayed at the enlightening information, Mike stares while Eli sets the tool aside and continues to sort through the mechanic chest. "Eli, how did you know John was still alive?"

Without looking up, the old farmer continues digging through his drawer of tools. "He came by here that night."

Mike tries to put it together. "Earlier that night?"

"Nope, it was pretty late, after it happened."

"Why did he come here?"

Twisting a socket wrench in his hand, Eli turns to Mike and winks. "Once upon a time, he worked summers here." The ratcheting click of the wrench stops, as Eli tells his version of the story. "When he came by here that night, he was pretty busted up. Took a real good beating alright. I patched him up best I could, 'fore I got him out of town."

"Busted up from what?"

"Don't know… He didn't say."

"How injured was he?"

Eli is silent a brief moment, as he thinks back and remembers the long-ago encounter. "I remember his face got the worst of it… Torn-up bad and a few busted ribs, I think. He'd been worked-over real good."

Mike listens intently, and can't believe what he's hearing. "Where did you send him off to?"

"He said he had to get out of town for a while, so I took him up to my sister's place."

"Did he give any hint as to what happened?"

Cicada

"Poor kid had a hard time gettin' words out on account of the busted jaw, but he managed to say that shit had gone bad, and he had to get away from town and Russling."

"Why?"

Eli looks at the deputy straight on and spits aside. "Cause ol' Russling's a no account, soft-puckered muff-diver. No offense to your mother 'n all." Mike nods his agreement, but can't seem to wrap his head around this series of events.

"But, why did John leave town?"

The farmer looks at the deputy and chuckles. "Well, if you're familiar with what happened the next day, you can probably figure it out for yourself."

"I was away from town at school during all of this and I couldn't make it back for a few weeks."

Eli grunts and looks around, noticing the cracks of sunlight streaming in from outside the barn. "Well, the situation got real peculiar, real fast, and the town just kinder shut down about it after that."

"Do you know where John is living now?"

Eli hesitates and then turns to his workbench. "Yep, sure do."

"Why haven't you told anyone this before?"

"Like I said, no one asked me."

The farmer goes back to his task, and Mike listens to the tools clanking on the bench. His thoughts reel, as events swirl in his head and slowly fall into place.

~*~

As the squad car drives into Burlingview, Mike begins to view his rural birthplace in a completely different light. Instead of the homegrown happiness he thought he grew up with, a sense of fear and trepidation seems to emanate from the isolated community. Driving down the quiet street, he glances at the voice recorder and the scribbles on his note pad. He turns into a driveway and pulls up to his own house.

After entering through the front door of the sparsely-furnished home, Mike crosses the living room to the kitchen. He weaves around some still-unpacked moving boxes and sees a message blink on the telephone answering machine. Breaking the silence of the room, he hits 'Play' on the device: *"Hey, Sweetie. I heard about your Uncle. Sticky was a good man, much like your father when they was younger. Stop on by if you need anything, or I'll just bring over some meals. Oh, I heard something else… We have to talk. Be good, Honey. Bye."*

As the message plays out, Mike sees a yellow, manila file envelope that has been slid under the back kitchen door. He picks up the package and peers out the door's window. Glancing around the empty alleyway, he pulls the curtain over the window and considers the envelope in his hand.

Curious, he takes the mysterious package to the living room couch, sits, and then unseals the flap. He slides the contents out across his lap and stares at a photocopied version of Russling's original police report files. He looks through the papers, peeks inside the envelope for some sort of message or note, and looks over his shoulder toward the kitchen door.

Chapter 26

Seventeen years prior …

Mrs. Connolly, lit by the glow of the flickering television set as she lies nude on the couch, hears the front door closing and raises her head to look around. She listens to faint footsteps on gravel driveway and a car door opening, then clicking shut. As the automobile's engine starts up, she sighs and lies her head back down.

~*~

Frank sleeps on the passenger-side seat of the police car with his head tilted on his shoulder, in an awkward position. Next to him in the car, Deputy Dodds sits half-awake behind the steering wheel. Between sleepy nods of his head, he keeps a steady watch on the house trailer. Suddenly, Dodds jerks awake when a set of car headlights blink on in the driveway. Through the patrol vehicle's dirty windshield, the deputy watches as the back-up lights flash on and the unknown car reverses down the driveway. "Wake up Frank, he's moving." Frank snorts awake and watches sleepily, as the car's lights sweep past the trailer and turn away toward town.

The deputy grabs the radio receiver from its clip on the dashboard. He clicks the trigger and takes a breath before speaking quietly into the mouthpiece. "Sheriff Russling...?" The radio is silent. The deputy heaves a sigh, and then a distant voice comes on the air.

"Go ahead, Dodds."

Deputy Dodds glances over to Frank and clicks the receiver again. "Suspect is on the move."

The sheriff responds, "I'm less than ten minutes away. Tail suspect until further notice."

"Copy that." Dodds starts the car and, as he clips the handheld receiver back on the dash clip, looks over at his civilian passenger. "Put on your seatbelt, Frank. Keep quiet." Dodds puts the car in gear and pulls out onto the road, following after the suspect.

~*~

The sheriff's patrol car speeds down the country road with its high-beam headlights lighting up the roadway from shoulder to shoulder. An occasional bush in the ditch or fencerow tree catches the wide beam of light as he races toward the Connolly trailer, just outside of town. The sheriff's tires skid, kicking gravel out the side, as they make the turn into the narrow driveway.

Sheriff Russling speeds up the lane, stops his car next to one of the parked cars and swings his door open. He leaves the engine running, as he jumps out and runs to the front porch of the moonlit trailer. His heavy frame pounds up the wooden staircase and he charges through the unlocked door.

The sheriff stands in the doorway, heaving for breath and scanning the room. He observes what he had already suspected. His new wife lies face down on the couch, completely naked and unconscious. With a bloody scrape on her back, it appears that she has conceivably been assaulted. He looks to the broken lamp on the floor, next to a pile of discarded clothing, and the television set that continues to cast its blue glow across the scene.

The sheriff swallows the rising lump in his throat, before bellowing loudly, "What in holy-hell happened?" Seething rage begins to boil as he assesses the situation.

A cool surge of night air enters through the open front door, waking Mrs. Connolly. Her head delicately rises from the couch pillow, and she looks at the sheriff through a drunken haze. A slight murmur escapes her lips, revealing the level of her intoxication, and he shakes his head in disgust. "Drunken whore..."

The sheriff exits the trailer, slamming the door shut behind him, as he trots to his car.

~*~

Frank and Deputy Dodds ride quietly in the patrol car, illuminated by the dashboard lights as they follow the car ahead in the distance. The red glowing orb of tail lights follow the contour of the winding road, out of reach of the police car's headlights. A crackle of static emits from the car radio and the voice of the sheriff interrupts. "Deputy Dodds..."

The deputy looks pensively to his ride-along passenger and then lifts the handset from the clip on the dashboard. "Dodds here. Go ahead, Sheriff."

"Are you still in visual contact with the suspect?"

Dodds clicks the radio and replies, "Yes, Sir."

"Detain that vehicle and give me your twenty."

There is a brief pause in radio communication, and the deputy makes another nervous glance over at his passenger. He reaches to the vehicle's console and flips on the light bar. The patrol car's front hood reflects the flashing blue and red police lights from the rooftop panel, and the deputy replies, "We are at the town limits, by the corner of Main and Ridge."

The radio crackles with static, and then the sheriff's voice announces. "Be there in five. Over."

Frank uncomfortably watches Dodds, as the deputy replaces the radio receiver on the dash clip, and they quickly close on the unidentified vehicle ahead. The flashing lights come up behind and both cars move to the gravel shoulder of the road. Dodds looks over to Frank and gives him a warning. "Stay here, Frank." With the engine and light bar still running, he opens his door, puts a leg out and turns to look back to his lone passenger. "It would be best if Russling didn't see you."

Heeding the deputy's parting words of warning, Frank slinks low in the passenger seat of the patrol car. He watches Deputy Dodds keep his hand placed on his sidearm, as he cautiously approaches the driver side of the detained vehicle. The deputy bends down to talk through the open window, and then he reaches out to receive the driver's license from the vehicle's operator.

Cicada

Dodds keeps a hand on the butt of his holstered pistol, as Frank watches through the dirty, bug-flecked windshield. The deputy tilts the small card to briefly examine the photo identification, using the flashing light from the police vehicle. Acknowledging with a nod, the officer turns over the driver's license card and taps it on the rolled-down window.

The identification is handed back through the window. The police deputy visibly relaxes and removes his palm from the handle of his revolver. To Frank's surprise, Deputy Dodds rests an arm above the door frame and socially chats with the unknown driver through the window.

With a roaring engine and the screeching of tires, the sheriff's police cruiser races down the middle of the roadway. The brakes lock up and the rear tires smoke rubber skids across the pavement as the sheriff's car angles in front of the deputy's parked vehicle.

Frank slinks down even further in his seat, murmuring to himself, "Oh, shit… This is not good."

Chapter 27

Through the back entrance, someone enters Mike Connolly's house and steps through the kitchen. Most of the window shades in the house are drawn, blocking out the yellow glow of light from the afternoon sun. Stepping around stacks of cardboard moving boxes, the figure moves quietly down the hallway, peering through open doorways as he goes.

In the bedroom, at the end of the hall, a look inside reveals Mike lying face down on the mattress, next to a pad of notes and small voice recorder. The unexpected touch of a hand causes Mike to wake with a jolt and roll from the bed.

In a tangle of blankets, Mike hits the floor hard, but manages to quickly draw out his police sidearm. "Who's here?!?"

Frank jumps back, his hands held high. "Hold on Mike! Don't shoot, dammit!"

Blinking his eyes awake, Mike slowly lowers his gun. "Frank, is that you?"

Frank slowly lowers his arms and steps forward into the rays of scattered sunlight streaming in from the window. "I tried to call, but your phone is out."

"What... It is?"

Disoriented, Mike pushes himself out from the tangle of blankets, climbs to his feet and looks around the bedroom. He picks up his notes and recorder, then moves past Frank and into the hall. The mechanic heaves a sigh and follows. "Do you have any idea at all what you're getting into, Mike?"

Mike turns around and stands with the notepad and recorder in one hand and his loaded firearm in the other. "Getting into what?"

Frank stares at Mike, and then lowers his voice down. "I'm talking about John... If you keep at it and Russling finds out I'm a witness, I'm a dead man."

"Did someone say something to you?"

"It's a small town, Mike."

The deputy places the recorder and notebook on the coffee table and then sits on the couch. Frank looks at the old-fashioned sheriff's badge on the table next to the pad of paper and then back to Mike. "Is that your dad's sheriff's badge?"

"Yeah. What of it?"

"Is this about him or John?"

"It's about John... And Russling."

Frank shakes his head. "He knows that there is something up."

Cicada

From the couch, Mike notices Frank's obvious discomfort as the mechanic glances to the windows. "Frank. I did tell Russling I knew what happened to Simms, but I didn't say how. Nobody else knows."

Frank's angst increases as he considers what Mike has just told him. He shakes his head, slides his hands into his hair and seems almost ready to cry. "Shit. I guess it doesn't matter anymore," he groans. "Why do you think he took Simms over to the garage to kill him?"

From the couch, Mike watches Frank go to the window, look out past the curtain and then anxiously touch the deadbolt lock on the front door. With his hand on the knob of the door, Frank hesitantly glances over his shoulder to Mike. "He knew there was a witness to what happened that night. Don't know if he knows for sure who it was, but he sure as hell was going to scare 'em into keeping their mouth shut."

"A witness to Hank Simm's murder?"

Frank stares at Mike and speaks in a low tone. "No. I'm talking about the murder of Deputy Dodds."

Mike wipes the lingering sleep from his eyes, as he attempts to comprehend what Frank is trying to communicate. "Who was the witness?"

Nervously, Frank looks around again and takes a slow, deliberate breath. "I saw him kill Deputy Dodds. Maybe was an accident, but he definitely did it."

Confused, Mike rubs his hand along the side of his face and asks Frank, "Russling killed his deputy?"

"I was there… In the car, before I went to hide."

"You were on the ride-along with Dodds?"

"Yes, and I think Russling might have seen me there that night... or, at least he suspects it."

Mike puts his fingers to his temples as he tries to think. "Why hasn't Russling ever said anything to you?"

"He didn't need to say a thing. Maybe he didn't see me, but he knew killing an innocent man as an example would keep everyone quiet mostly." Frank's tough exterior melts away as he continues. "He had it all wrapped up and figured, if he could keep this town scared, then no one would cause him any trouble."

Realizing the true depth of the situation, Mike looks at the pad of paper on the table and flips a page over before peering up at Frank. "Did you see the driver of the car?"

"No, but Dodds recognized him."

Confused, Mike grimaces. "So, why Hank Simms?" Frank looks through a gap in the front window curtain and adjusts his gaze nervously. "You will have to ask John that." Frank senses that Mike is beginning to understand.

The sound of a car pulling into the driveway turns their attention to the front of the house. Mike hops up from the couch, moves alongside Frank at the curtained window and peeks out to the street. A cold sweat suddenly comes over him as he recognizes the sheriff's car parking behind his own car. Mike takes a step back from the window and looks at Frank. "Go home. I'll talk to you later."

Frank nods his head in agreement and moves through the kitchen toward the back door. "Don't tell him anything. He's dangerous."

Cicada

Now fully awake, Mike looks to his old friend and waves him away. "I'll take care of it, Frank."

~*~

The car engine shuts off, and the sheriff steps out. Russling studies the deputy's vehicle before him and then up to the home's curtained windows. Moving around the car door, he nudges it shut with his hip, as he walks to the house. Passing Mike's patrol car in the driveway, he peeks through the window to see the John Bratcher file on the passenger seat. He turns back to the house when he hears the front door unlock and then open up.

Mike appears in the door, and Russling looks up, as the deputy steps out. "Hello Michael. Feeling better?"

Mustering up a phony smile, Mike steps outside to the front porch and greets Russling. "Trying to get some rest."

"That's good. You seemed upset this morning."

Mike chokes down his resentment and replies, "Yeah, I'm sorry. It was just my... Uh... my misunderstanding."

Now in an awkward stand-off, the sheriff assesses the deputy. "Today was a rough day for you, what with your Uncle's passing and all. Matters can sometimes get out of hand... We tend to lose focus when these things happen..."

Mike nods and waits for the intended meaning of the sheriff's visit. They quietly stare at each other until Mike asks, "Did you need to talk to me about something?"

Eric H. Heisner

"No. Just stopped by to see how you were doing. Your mother seemed worried about you, so I thought I'd check in."

At the mention of his mother, Mike is reminded of his conversation with her. Breaking into a nervous sweat, he responds, "I'm fine. What did she say?"

"Nothing much... Just that she was concerned for you." The sheriff glances again to the front seat of the squad car as he turns to leave. He pauses, stopping to look back at Mike. Reveling in the deputy's apparent unease, he adds smugly, "Why don't you take a few days off. Sort out your perspective on things..." After a pause, he continues. "You know, it's best not to dig in your own backyard. It can make a bit of a mess." The sheriff puts on an insincere smile, with dark undertones. "No telling what you'll find... Understand?"

Solemnly, Mike nods and replies, "Sure."

Russling eyes the deputy for a few seconds before stepping back to his car and pulling the driver-side door open. He gives a casual salute before sliding in and turning the key to start up the engine. Through the sun-glared windshield, Mike catches a slight, wicked grin from Russling before the sheriff looks over his shoulder to back up and drive away.

Chapter 28

Mike shuts the door to his patrol car, returns to the house with the stack of folders under his arm, and then goes inside. He sets the pile on the table, next to his notes, and begins to sort through the file papers. Frank steps out from the shadows and speaks, "He's sitting at the end of the street."

Mike nearly jumps out of his skin in shock. "Damn! What are you still doing here?"

Frank looks over Mike's shoulder at the file reports. "The last thing I want is for Russling to see me run out the back door while he is interrogating you."

"He wasn't interrogating me."

Frank shrugs and glances to the curtained windows. "That's what it looked like from here." He raises an eyebrow when he notices the recorder on the table next to the files. "Hell, he should be with you building this case against him. Are you going to be able to nail him with this?"

Uncertain, but wanting to appear confident for the sake of his friend, Mike picks up the notepad and voice recorder. He places them on top of the stack of folders and replies, "Depends if I can find John and get him back here to testify."

Frank circles the couch, moves to the front door and carefully takes another peek out through the window curtains. "Russling is just waiting for you to make a move like that."

"You drive here? Where is your truck parked?"

Frank glances behind and replies as Mike picks up the phone and begins to dial. "In the back alley."

Mike slowly puts the receiver back in its cradle and looks to Frank disconcertingly. "The phone is out…"

Frank returns the deputy's gaze with a concerned look. "Now you're starting to get it."

~*~

The pickup truck that usually sits parked in front of Frank's garage backs down the alley behind Mike's house. Mike scrunches down in the passenger seat, as Frank keeps a sharp eye out the rear window. The old transmission whines, as the vehicle rolls back in reverse. Bumping over the curb, Frank eases into the street and shifts to a low forward gear and the truck drives off.

The afternoon sun drops behind the buildings in town and long shadows consume the quiet street. Frank stops the truck in front of his shop, shifts to neutral and sets the brake. Looking over to his old high school friend crouched down low on the bench seat beside him, he mutters, "Stay here. I have to grab a few things."

Cicada

The aged truck creaks, as the door handle is pulled and the driver's-side door opens. Frank slides out, swings the door closed and notices a note taped to the entrance of his shop. Glancing back to Mike huddled low on the passenger seat, he walks to the garage and takes the note from the window.

His head lowered down, reading the handwritten note, Frank's hand begins to tremble. Tentatively, the mechanic walks back to the pickup truck and leans in on the open, driver's side window. Anxiously, Mike asks, "What is it? What's the matter?"

"A little message from Russling…"

"What does it say?"

Frank takes a deep breath and hands the note to Mike. "He knows what's up…"

After taking a moment to read the short message, Mike looks back to his nervous friend. "He can't connect you with anything I said to him."

"If I leave town with you, he'll know for sure."

Feeling helpless, Mike grits his teeth and implores, "Frank, I need your help to convince John to come back!"

Frank thinks, then gently shakes his head and glances apprehensively at the empty street. "You don't need my help. I need to stay around here, or he'll know what's up for sure."

Mike crumples up the note and tosses it to the floorboard. "Dammit! I don't care if he's the sheriff. I'm going to get the bastard for what he's done!"

Outside the truck window, Frank nods half-heartedly while rubbing his nose nervously and sniffing into his hand. "You've wanted to do this for a long time." He looks aside, expecting to see a police car turn the corner at any moment. "Why don't you take my truck and go find wherever John is. I'll stay here and hold down the fort in case Russling shows."

"Are you sure?"

"At least I can keep an eye on him for you."

"I'll find John and bring him back here."

"Yeah, you do that. Now, go on and get outta here." Frank backs away from the window and looks around again. "And hurry up, before he comes around here looking for you. I'll walk home and lay low."

The seat creaks as Mike slides over to the driver's side and gets situated behind the steering wheel. "What will you tell Russling if you see him?"

"I'll say I've been sick in bed and haven't seen you since you borrowed my truck for some vacation."

Mike turns the key to crank the engine on the pickup and glances over his shoulder, through the back window. "Watch yourself. I'll bring John back here and everything will work out." Frank gives Mike a half-hearted salute as the truck grinds into gear and the gas pedal is feathered to keep the engine from choking out.

Frank shrugs, "Yeah sure… everything will be fine." He watches warily as his friend drives down the street, turns the corner and disappears. Alone in front of the repair garage, Frank murmurs aloud, "I sure as hell hope so."

Chapter 29

The truck headlights guide Mike through the darkness of a moonless night, as he travels down a two-lane rural highway. The glow from the dashboard illuminates Mike's features, as he stares ahead, occasionally glancing to the stack of folders spread across the passenger seat. The comforting rumble of the old truck's engine puts the deputy into a meditative state. Mike stares straight ahead, mentally piecing together the tragic events that led to the disappearance of an old friend.

~*~

Early the next morning, the pickup truck is parked at a roadside motel surrounded by farm fields. It is cloaked in a layer of dew, as are the other vehicles lined up before a row of closed doors. The chiming ring of a small bell over a doorway breaks the stillness and Mike exits the motel office. He looks at the scrap of paper in his hand as he walks to the truck.

After a few grinding cranks, the old truck starts up, and the wipers swipe away the moisture from the windshield. Mike checks over his shoulder, while he backs into the street. A haze of exhaust spills from the tailpipe and disperses into the chilly morning air. Still holding the small slip of paper, Mike glances at the scribbled note and murmurs, "I hope I can find him at this address." He presses his foot to the gas pedal, as he turns the steering wheel and drives off down the road.

~*~

The pickup truck drives up to a farmstead with a long gravel driveway and the vehicle creaks to an idling stop. Numbers for the home address can be seen on the round-top metal mailbox, perched on a wooden post in need of repair. The truck engine rumbles at a low idle and the morning sun glistens at the edges of the dirt shrouded windshield.

Mike looks down at the numbers on the slip of paper again and compares them to the address on the old mailbox. He takes a hesitant breath and lifts his foot from the brake. Turning the steering wheel, he drives the truck down the lane to the farmstead with its barn and numerous outbuildings. The truck rolls on the gravel path and nervous tension grips Mike's features, as he visualizes a reunion with the friend he had previously assumed to be deceased. The pickup truck stops before the screened porch of the farmhouse and Mike turns off the ignition key. He gazes out at the quiet homestead and listens to the soft rustle of tree leaves blowing in the wind and the squeak from the hinge on the screen door.

Cicada

Finally, he pushes open the truck door, steps out and walks up to the house.

After not finding any sort of doorbell, Mike reaches out to knock on the wood-frame of the screen door. He glances around the porch and waits a moment before calling out. "Hello... Is there anyone at home?" After a minute of stillness, he knocks again and leans in closer to the door to listen if he can hear anyone inside the house.

Not getting any response, from inside the house, Mike walks back to the truck and hears the pinging sound of metalworking coming from one of the barn-style outbuildings. As he walks across the gravel lot that connects the house to the various outbuildings, he hears an air compressor kick on. Approaching the open sliding doors at the side of the long shed, he peers inside. The compressor tank triggers the automatic shut-off and all is suddenly quiet again.

"Hello...?" Across the dirt-floored shed, Mike hears the clanking of tools being set down, then looks in that direction. "Is anyone around?"

An older man in filthy work clothes steps into a lit area near a workbench and stares toward Mike at the doorway. With craggy features that put his age in the sixties, Henry Garvin appears to be a mechanic interrupted from his work. Holding a welding mask in his dust-stained hands, he glances back at the workbench before asking, "What kin I do you for?"

Mike steps into the shed to let his eyes adjust better to the dim light. He studies the assortment of farm equipment machinery in the shop and then turns back to the mechanic. "I'm looking for a friend." The mechanic nods but doesn't speak. Sensing Henry's ambivalence, Mike explains further. "His name is John Bratcher."

Henry lowers his chin and sets his welding helmet down on the workbench. "Never heard of 'im."

Mike takes another step inside and continues his query. "He moved up this way a few years ago." Mike watches the mechanic continue his chore at the shop workbench, not seeming to pay much attention to him. "Actually, it was about seventeen years ago…"

Henry glares over his shoulder at Mike before turning back to his workbench. In a gruff voice he repeats himself, "Said, never heard of him."

"Could I ask you a few questions?"

"No."

"Why?"

"I've got work to do."

Mike takes a chance and presses the mechanic with another probing question. "Do you think anyone in town might know of him or how to get in contact with him?" Without looking back, the mechanic shrugs and moves off to a dim corner of the shop.

Mike stands and waits a while before turning to leave. He steps out of the cool, dimly-lit barn back into the sunlight, and his eyes readjust to the brightness. He notices that, with exception of his truck and the quiet drone of a low-flying airplane in the distance the rural farmstead seems almost abandoned.

Mike walks back to the truck, and pulls open the door. He looks back at the farm house, studying each window, half-expecting to see a ghost from his past

Cicada

peering back at him. Disappointed, Mike slides into the truck, tugs the door with a creaking groan and starts the engine. The door clicks closed with a bang of metal and Mike puts the truck in gear. The soft crunch of gravel is heard as the vehicle rolls down the lane.

At the end of the driveway, Mike is about to turn onto the roadway when the drone of the airplane gets louder, attracting his attention. From behind a fence-row of tall trees, the crop-dusting plane leaps over the top and dives down for a grass-strip landing that takes it to the open-door side of the long shed. At the end of the driveway, Mike watches as the mechanic steps out from the barn and approaches the aircraft.

After a brief conversation with Henry, the pilot revs the plane's single engine. The aircraft pivots around, as Henry Garvin hobbles back to the open doorway of the barn to watch as the small airplane taxies, picks up sped and nimbly leaps into the air.

Mike glances down at the police files stacked beside him on the bench seat and back to the farm buildings again. He bends low, watching the airplane climb into the sky and then gazes over to the mechanic in the doorway of the barn. "What's that old coot up to?" Releasing the brake pedal and pressing on the gas, Mike pulls out into the roadway and drives parallel to the farm buildings. Again, he looks to the stack of files and the small slip of paper with the address scribbled on it. Mike drives down the country road and contemplates his next move.

Suddenly, Mike hears the loud roaring of an engine, and the crop-dusting airplane dives right over the roadway, directly in front of the moving truck. He swerves aside and stops the truck just short of the ditch. "Holy-crap! What in..." He kicks open the door, hops out and watches, as the aircraft opens up its sprayers to dust the length of a leafy, green field.

Roadside, the truck sits canted down toward the ditch. Standing by the open door of the truck, Mike watches the aircraft bank at the end of the crop row, fly under a low-slung set of power lines and do another pattern of in-flight dusting. As Mike looks back down the gravel road toward the farmstead, he notices a yellow, diamond-shaped warning sign that reads: *Caution, low flying aircraft.*

With a sigh, he murmurs to himself, "If I chose to disappear, this sure would be the place to do it."

Chapter 30

Seated on the metal porch chairs outside the roadside motel, Mike scans the small squiggles of writing on his pad of paper. On the table next to him are a bottle of beer, the files and his voice recorder. The motel owner comes out from the main office and walks over to Mike, who appears to be lost in concentration. He stops and watches the new guest until Mike finally breaks from his train of thought and looks up at him.

The motel owner scratches under and around his arm, spits to the side and squints. "You a lawyer or somethin'?"

A bit startled, Mike shuffles his papers and answers. "Uh, no... Just doing some research."

"What fer?"

"I'm trying to help an old friend."

"Yeah? Who?"

Mike gives a placating smile as he tucks the file papers away and closes up the police reports spread over his lap. "You wouldn't, by any chance, know a fella, John Bratcher?"

The motel owner thinks, and then flashes a wide grin. "Nope." He scrapes a fingernail on his front tooth and grunts. "Ask me 'bout anyone else hereabouts, and I likely know 'em. I'm proud to know about everyone that's worth knowing." The motel owner sucks food from his teeth and continues, "Heck, the residents 'round here pretty much stay the same. You kin jest 'bout bet on when an unexpected baby is born, some young feller will be skipping out of town real fast. Kinder evens things out."

Entertained, Mike sits back in the rusty chair, lets the motel keeper's rambling chatter sink in, and smiles. Realizing he might have an attentive audience, the old man perks up. "Go ahead…Ask me 'bout anyone else. I bet I know 'em."

"How about Eli Warren?

"Yep, his sister lives just down the road."

Mike thinks, and has an idea that could be a long shot. "Do you know the pilot from the farm over yonder that does the crop dusting?"

"Sure. He's the new feller."

Mike nods, returns to his notes and murmurs aloud, "The new guy, huh? John moved here quite a few years ago." The motel owner watches as Mike flips to the next folder, opens it and puts his notepad alongside. Catching the hint to leave Mike alone, the motel owner takes a step away and stops to scratch at a piece of chewing gum on the sidewalk. Concentrating on the dark spot on the concrete, he adds, "Yep... Arrived about fifteen, maybe twenty years ago."

Mike has a surge of excitement. "How old is he?"

The motel owner stops picking at the gum and thinks. "Well... younger than me. Dunno, probably closer to yer age."

Mike abruptly stands up from the metal chair and takes the stack of files back to his room. He quickly returns with the truck keys and his coat.

He rushes past the motel owner, still scratching at the old chewing-gum on the sidewalk, and calls out, "Good talking to you. See ya later."

The man toes the dark spot and watches him go. "Sure. Anytime... Ya jest let me know if you wants to know 'bout anyone else. I'll probably remember 'em."

The truck starts up, reverses from the motel parking lot, and barks a rear tire as it drives off. The motel owner is bewildered by the guest's sudden exit and watches as the old pickup truck drives off down the road. The motel owner looks again to the dark stain on the sidewalk, shrugs and walks back to the main office.

~*~

The two-lane county road leading to the farmstead is deserted. Mike keeps his eyes to the sky as he approaches, half-expecting to see the crop-dusting airplane dive down at him again. Turning at the mailbox, the truck drives down the gravel lane, kicking up a trailing haze of dust in its wake.

Mike drives past the vacant farm house and pulls in front of the open, double sliding doors of the machine shed. The truck turns off and the dusty wheels crunch to a stop. Sliding out of the pickup, Mike calls out to anyone that might be inside the barn, "Hello…?"

The mechanic appears in the doorway and grimaces when he sees Mike. "You again? What do you want now?"

Mike walks up to Henry, stops and peers past the mechanic's shoulder to the cool, dark interior of the building. "Just need a minute. I want to speak to that pilot of yours."

"Is that so… What fer?"

Mike lets his eyes scan the farmstead and replies, "He nearly ran me off the road this afternoon."

Henry glances at the afternoon sky and huffs, "And yer just mentioning it now?"

"It just started to bother me."

Henry nods and flips the flathead screwdriver he was holding into the air. He catches it by the handle and then uses the flat tip to scratch around behind his opposite upper arm. "He didn't mention it."

Mike studies the dubious mechanic's wary demeanor. "Is he here?" He attempts to hide his mounting excitement as he adds, "I would really like to talk with him."

"He's gone."

"Until when?"

"He won't be around any tonight."

"Will he be back tomorrow?"

Henry heaves a sigh and twirls the long screwdriver. "He said if you come by again lookin' for him, to tell you to meet him at the coffee shop tomorrow morning at six o'clock."

Cicada

"He said what?"

Henry flips the flathead screwdriver, end over end, catches it, turns away and grumbles, "You heard me okay." The mechanic steps back into the dimly-lit, machine shed and disappears behind a large piece of farming equipment. Standing alone in the open doorway, Mike gets a strong sensation that he is on the verge of discovery.

Chapter 31

The only coffee shop in town clamors with the usual early morning business. Mike sits alone in one of the middle booths. Staring at the front entry, he shifts his feet, impatiently watching the entrance of each patron. With each chiming jingle of the bells on the door handle, his heart nearly leaps from his chest. He looks at the big, round clock face above the breakfast counter and notices the time is almost a quarter past the hour. "Damn… What am I even doing here?"

The waitress walks over with a pot of coffee and reaches to refill Mike's cup. "Did you say something?"

Slightly embarrassed at be caught talking to himself, he glances up at her and nods his thanks as she tops off his mug. "No. I'm just waiting on a friend."

She smiles kindly and looks around the restaurant. "Can I get you anything else while you wait?

"No, thank you. Not that hungry just yet…"

Mike gives her a pleasant smile and lets his attention return to the front entrance. As the waitress moves away, someone brushes past her. The man passes, bumps Mike's arm and slips into the seat on the opposite side of the table. Awestruck, Mike stares at the aged and scarred face of his school friend, John Bratcher.

"Hello, Mike. It's been a long time."

~*~

Frank's pickup truck drives down a country highway. Mike drives silently, while John stares out the window, casting his gaze to the streaming line of unkempt fencerow. The countryside rolls past, as they drive down the two-lane blacktop. John glances beside to Mike and looks away. "I told you… I can't go back."

Mike stares ahead, avoiding the sight of healed scars on John's time-worn features. "I need your help to nail Russling."

John peers down at the pile of police report folders and file papers between them on the seat. "Mike, You don't have enough here to do anything. All you have is a discrepancy concerning a date."

The truck continues to roll along the country road as Mike turns to look at John. "Your testimony would seal it." John sees his friend face forward to watch the road again. Heavy-hearted, he glances to the stack of folders, grits his teeth, shakes his head and sighs.

~*~

The old pickup truck pulls up to the rural farm house, drives past, and stops in front of the machine shed. The motor continues to run as the two friends sit silently in the truck cab. Mike finally turns to face John.

Cicada

After studying the raised scarring on John's cheek, he clears his throat with a cough. "Are you coming back with me?"

Conflicted, John continues to stare forward. The scar on his cheek twitches. His mouth dry, trying to swallow the lump rising in his throat, he turns to Mike. "How much do you really know about what happened?"

"I know enough to get him."

John pauses then takes a breath and barely whispers, "No, I mean the other stuff. The things about your mother…?"

Mike studies the face of his long-time friend, searching for answers. "I know about it… She told me."

John seems confused. "She did?"

Mike nods certain. "Yes, she told me she wasn't assaulted that night."

Disconcerted, John turns to Mike. He looks closely at the friend he grew up with, relieved to see there isn't any hostility toward him. John shakes his head apologetically. "I'm so sorry for what I did."

"It's okay."

A heavy silence follows their difficult exchange. Then, John wipes his tear-filled eyes and hesitantly asks, "Why…?" His chin trembles and he tries to look up to meet Mike's gaze. "Knowing all this, why would you want me to come back?"

Mike stares directly at his long-lost friend. "You're my friend. You have a life to get back to."

John lowers his head and wobbles it despondently. "Not anymore. My parents live there, but once they're gone, there isn't anything to make me ever want to go back." John tilts his head with remorse and slowly turns to Mike. "Why don't you just let it alone?"

Mike stares back at John, surprised at his reluctance. "Why is everyone so afraid to stand up? I can't just let it go."

John rests both of his hands on his lap, then clenches them and turns to the window. "I'm alive… You found me. What's it matter, one way or the other?"

Becoming a bit agitated by John's unwillingness to help, Mike continues to press his friend. "Russling cannot be allowed to cover this up… He's a murderer."

"It's not that simple."

"He can't get away with it!"

Thinking he shouldn't have to be working this hard to convince his friend to bring justice to the person who ruined his life, Mike is exasperated. "Who knows who else he would hurt or intimidate to keep these things from coming out." Mike pounds his fist on the stack of file folders between them. "He's going to have to answer for his actions!"

John looks at his upset friend and studies him intently. "There isn't just one person that's guilty here."

"What do you mean?"

Aggravated, John sighs heavily and shakes his head. "The whole town knows how Russling is. If they wanted to get rid of him, they would have done it a long time ago." Their eyes locked on each other, John frowns at his old friend. "You're in over your head… You just need to let it be."

Mike looks away and huffs in disbelief. "I can't do that. Not now that I know how it really was."

Cicada

John is reluctant and responds, "Digging into the past isn't going to heal old wounds. Your father isn't coming back, and you can't change that by fixing Russling or bringing up what happened that night."

John pulls on the handle by the armrest and pushes the truck door open. "There are a lot of people affected here."

Mike nods. "I'm heading back tomorrow."

On the edge of the bench seat, halfway out the door, John slumps his shoulders and glances away, downhearted. "I'll go and do whatever you ask… I owe you that much."

Relieved, Mike inhales deeply and relaxes his clenched fist on the stack of folders. "What time should I pick you up?"

John steps out from the pickup and stands by the door. He looks at the police deputy who was once his close friend. "Come by in the morning, and I'll tell them I need to take some time off."

Mike replies, "You won't regret it."

John swings the door shut and stares at Mike through the passenger window. "It's too late for that."

Chapter 32

The first rays of the morning sun rise over long rows of planted fields. Under a blanket of dew that reflects the light of a new day, the pickup truck drives down the country road. The air seems fresh and new, despite the anticipated return. Inside the cab of the truck, Mike and John sit silently observing the outside world as it passes by the windows. Mike looks ahead at the roadway, occasionally glancing at the somber friend sitting beside him. He notices how the nervous passenger squeezes the armrest with clenched fingers that repeatedly grip and release. Mike contemplates a question, but stifles it and looks back to the empty highway ahead.

On the passenger side, John restlessly fidgets until the suspenseful quietness inside the truck is almost unbearable. Mike glances at John, looks back to the roadway and mutters, "What did you mean yesterday?"

"When?"

Mike watches the road and replies, "You said, it was too late, and that others were guilty."

The question unsettles John. He takes a moment then utters a reluctant reply. "I regret everything that happened that night, and I'm sorry for everything that followed."

Mike senses the opportunity for more answers and presses further. "What did happen, exactly?"

Feeling powerless to stop things, John stares forward, looking out the truck window. "I still don't know exactly. Nothing that made any sense."

Mike realizes that John is trembling, and tries to be sensitive as he continues his inquiry. "We can start with what I know." He receives a subtle nod from John. The deputy gestures to the first page of notes on the stack of open files. "You stopped by the bar when you got into town?"

John takes a deep breath and gulps before answering, "I had a few drinks with the guys."

Mike adds, "Then you drove to my place to see if I was home?"

John sits silent and watches out the side window. Adjusting his grip on the wheel, Mike gives him a moment. The uncomfortable silence returns, but the deputy presses on. "Is that correct?"

"Yes."

"How long were you there?"

"I don't know. I had a few drinks there, too."

Mike glimpses down at his notepad and then to John. "After that, what happened?" Beads of sweat begin

Cicada

to glisten on John's temple and he wipes it away with the tips of his trembling fingers. "I was heading home."

The deputy stares down the length of road before them and speaks to his passenger. "And you just chanced to drive by where Russling killed Deputy Dodds at the edge of town?"

John's chin begins to tremble, and he looks at Mike. "Wha... What...?"

The deputy takes his eyes from the road for a second to look down at the file folders, the recorder and his pile of notes. A tension fills the air as Mike repeats his presumptions regarding the unfolding of events that night. "Along the road, at the edge of town, you caught Russling in the act... Right?"

John breathes heavily, shakes his head and mumbles, "That's not exactly right."

As Mike continues driving, he pulls the notes to his lap. He quickly glimpses down at them, and then glances at John. "I figured out that much. I assumed you stopped to help Dodds... But it was too late, and Russling came at you next?" John sits pale and sweating, but doesn't interject as Mike finishes his assessment. "What I don't yet understand is why Russling killed his own deputy? He must've had something on the sheriff that he didn't want out."

John writhes in the seat, clenches his jaw and replies, "He was only trying to help."

"Help who?"

Mike looks over and notices there is a pained look of fearful remorse filling his friend's features as

John responds. "Me... He just got in the way, and Russling killed him."

"How?"

John takes a deep, trembling breath and explains, "Deputy Dodds pulled me over after leaving your place, and Russling showed up shortly after." Angst twitches the jagged scar on John's cheek as he completes his declaration of guilt. "Mike... I didn't rape your mother."

"Yes, I know that. She told me she wasn't assaulted." Mike looks at his uneasy friend curiously, and then continues, "I figured Russling put that in to frame Simms?"

There is an awkward moment as John starts to realize his actual meaning isn't coming across very well. He tries to stop the trembling of his hands and stares out through the insect-smeared windshield. "She was with me that night... That's what put Russling into the rage."

Mike takes his attention from the road ahead and looks inquisitively at his anxious passenger. "What do you mean?"

John apprehensively bites his lip, as he watches Mike wrestle with the concept of what he is trying to explain. Apologetically, he faces his friend and confesses the truth. "That night, I was with your mother."

Mike receives the unexpected information like a hammer-punch to the gut. He nearly lets the truck wander off the roadway, but quickly swerves back and regains control. Finding it hard to believe what he just heard, he merely gasps, "What are you saying?"

Cicada

John glances to the handle on the truck door and contemplates bailing out, but realizes he is past the point of no return. "We didn't mean for it to happen."

The disillusioned deputy bears down and grips the steering wheel so hard that the knuckles on his hand turn pale. He makes an effort to control the feelings of betrayal while his friend attempts to explain, "It just happened…"

The emotionally-pained deputy puts out an open palm to silence John. "Alright…! Shut up!" He clenches his jaw tighter and slings the notepad from his lap to the floorboard. John scoots his body closer to the door and almost whimpers, "I thought you knew?"

With both hands on the wheel, Mike glares at John with an uncharacteristic, angry-rage in his eyes. "Shut the hell up… Not another word!" He slams his fist against the wheel and grips it tighter, as he stares ahead. John watches the fuming deputy with pangs of familiar dread. An uncomfortable silence is all that follows.

Chapter 33

The pickup truck pulls in front of *Frank's Transmission and Repair* and rolls to a groaning stop. Waiting for instructions, John studies the shop building he remembers from long ago. Mike faces forward and, without looking over, he mutters, "Go in and tell Frank to pack some things." Mike continues to keep his gaze focused ahead. "I'll be back to pick you both up. I have to grab some stuff."

"Where are we going?"

Mike responds coolly, without turning to look at John. "We'll have to go outside of this township to get protection. We need help with this." He pauses and unclenches his jaw. "Things aren't what I thought they were." John solemnly nods, swings open the truck door and steps out into the street. He looks across the cab to his upset friend. "I'm sorry, Mike."

The deputy stares ahead, not accepting the apology. John takes a step back from the vehicle and pushes the door closed with a gentle click. Mike steps on the gas and roars off. Standing across from the repair garage, in his old hometown, John feels extremely out of place and vulnerable.

Alone and unsure, John approaches the entrance of the transmission shop and notices the 'Closed' sign in the window. He twists the door handle and finds it locked. Peering through the window, he detects a single light at the back of the garage.

"That's just great…"

He makes his way around the repair shop, approaches the rear entrance door and notices that the window is broken. He touches the levered handle and the damaged door slowly swings inward. The smell of oil and gas fumes waft outside and John freezes as a rush of terror sweeps through him.

Seventeen years prior …

The shining beams of headlights and the strobing flash of police emergency lights cut into the darkness all around. Sheriff Russling swings his car door open and jumps out with a pump shotgun in his hand. He walks briskly toward the vehicle on the shoulder of the road and forcefully shoves Deputy Dodds aside. Bending to peer inside the stopped car, the sheriff bellows loudly, "Get out of the vehicle." He puts the hand without the shotgun to the open window frame and glares in at the driver. "Now!"

Cicada

Behind the sheriff, Deputy Dodds stumbles back against the rear panel of the car. The deputy is astounded as the sheriff grips the shotgun with both hands and jabs the stock through the open window to hit the driver in the face. He reaches out to grab the shotgun from the hands of the officer and yells, "Hold it, Sheriff!"

Russling shoves the pleading deputy away and jerks the chrome handle outward to swing the driver's door open. He drags the stunned driver out from behind the steering wheel and throws him to the center-line of the rural highway. In a rage, the sheriff smacks the victim several times with the wooden stock of the shotgun and kicks him in the head. Beaten and bloodied, the abused driver lies curled in the middle of the roadway, defenseless.

The stunned deputy steps up and aggressively pulls the law officer away. "Sheriff, what the hell are you doing?" Dodds grabs hold of the shotgun's barrel and tries to keep the sheriff from smacking it on the grounded victim. "Stop it!"

In a blind rage, Russling jerks the gun away from the deputy's grip and kicks a booted foot out to the curled body on the ground. His kick connects with a bone crunching crack, and the driver whimpers, coughing blood onto the pavement. Deputy Dodds retains his grip on the sheriff's sleeve and continues trying to pull him off. "Sheriff, you got to stop this!"

Russling turns on the deputy and vehemently shoves him down across the front fender of the stopped vehicle. During a moment of pause, Russling looks at Dodds gawking back at him and jacks the shotgun with a one-handed pump. A loaded shell inserts into the chamber, and the sheriff turns his attentions back to the beaten driver, curled in the roadway. "This son-of-a-bitch was with my wife!"

The driver on the ground coughs up a spattering of blood and slowly turns his head around to look at the sheriff. John's features are barely recognizable due to the bleeding lacerations from the brutal strikes. Russling lifts the stock of the short-barreled riot gun to his shoulder and glares down at the cowering young man. A faint glimmer of a smirk crosses his lips, as his finger pokes through the trigger guard and starts to squeeze.

Regaining his balance, Deputy Dodds lunges at the sheriff and attempts to pull the aimed shotgun barrel away. The sheriff pivots his stance, and a muffled blast from the shotgun explodes into the deputy's midsection, point blank. An expression of pain and shock appears fleetingly on the deputy's face, as he stumbles back against the rear panel of the roadside vehicle.

As Deputy Dodds crumples into a lifeless heap, the sheriff stands unexpectedly calm following his fit of hostility. He looks down at the young man from the stopped vehicle, spitting bloody saliva and gasping for breath, and then looks back to his deputy's seemingly empty squad car.

Outwardly calm and collected, Russling pumps the forestock of the firearm to eject the remaining shot shells and picks up the unfired casings, one by one, from the roadway. He tucks them in his pocket and, with a rattling scratch of metal on pavement, sets the empty shotgun down in the road next to the driver. With his handkerchief, he carefully wipes the receiver and trigger area of the shotgun for fingerprints.

Still coughing and gasping for air, John Bratcher remains curled in the roadway, as the sheriff takes his opened hand and presses it around the receiver and trigger guard. Looming over the heaving form, Russling appears satisfied, and then walks past the dead deputy and around to the open door of his squad car. He reaches inside for the police radio, clicks the button on the handset and barks, "Control, this is Sheriff Russling…"

Suddenly, the sheriff's peripheral vision catches the interior overhead light of the deputy's patrol car blink on. Instantly dropping the radio handset to the seat, he draws his sidearm and focuses his attention on the deputy's vehicle. Moving around the front of his police car, Sheriff Russling passes through the beam of the headlights, casting a long shadow down the roadway and across the curled bodies hunched near the pulled-over car and incriminating shotgun. The sheriff advances on the deputy's squad car, as the red glow from the light bar strobes his figure. His boot soles scuff on the pavement, as he moves forward. With his pistol ready, Sheriff Russling calls out to the seemingly empty vehicle, "Who's there?"

Russling continues forward and steps around the open passenger door to take a look inside. He points his handgun, ready to shoot, and sees an unoccupied vehicle. The sheriff reaches in to take a flashlight from the dash, clicks it on and scans the empty back seat.

Not finding anyone inside, he slams the door closed. Shining the white beam of the flashlight over the

Eric H. Heisner

empty ditch and out to the rural landscape beyond, Russling holds his pistol aim just below the light as he searches the dark night. "Come out, or I'll find you later..." With pistol still in hand, Sheriff Russling clicks the flashlight off and steps back to his waiting vehicle.

He walks toward the front of the idling patrol car and looks out into the wide-reaching spread of car headlights to see Deputy Dodds slumped dead, lying in a pool of blood, against the rear fender of the stopped car. As the police strobe lights continue to flash, Russling's gaze moves to the center of the roadway, where he sees only the empty shotgun and a splatter of coughed-up blood on the pavement. Everything is deathly still, until the swelling chatter of cicadas rises to a nearly deafening pitch.

Chapter 34

The inside of Frank's repair shop is dark but for the light of a single bulb hanging over a work bench. There is the crunching sound of broken window glass underfoot, as John steps inside the doorway and looks around. He peers into the garage and calls out, "Frank? You around?"

Standing near the door, John reaches back against the wall and flips on the light switch. Overhead, the fluorescent bulbs start to flicker and a green glow of light fills the garage. John looks to a car positioned between the uprights of the auto-lift and another parked beside it, with its hood raised up. "Frank, are you here?" He walks around the cars toward the workbench and stops short.

Splayed out, in a pool of blood on the floor, is a body that appears to have been severely beaten around the head. The familiar feeling of horrible dread instantly consumes John, as he looks at the mangled, lifeless form of the mechanic. Slowly, he steps around to look at the victim's mashed face, and with a fleeting glimpse, recognizes who it is.

"Oh, Frank…"

John looks to a large monkey wrench on the concrete floor nearby with tufts of bloody hair clinging to the end of it. The memory of Deputy Dodds being shot point-blank in the road flashes through his mind. He backs away from the body and slips on something metal. John looks near his feet and spies an old fashioned sheriff's badge. He leans down to read the name on the badge: *Sheriff M. Connolly.*

A cold chill of terror overwhelms John, as he chokes back the rising vomit in his throat. The dead body on the floor, in a pooling of blood, and the grisly sight of Deputy Dodds, slumped against the panel of the car bursts into his thoughts. Gasping for a breath of air, John stutters back a few steps, bounces off the car fender, scrambles to the door and disappears into the darkness.

~*~

The afternoon light shines through the leaves on the trees, and the chattering of cicadas fills the air, as Frank's truck drives up the back alley and stops behind Mike's house. The truck engine shuts off, and Mike swings the creaking door open to get out. He quickly scans around the fenced-in yard, before walking toward the rear door that leads to the kitchen. Mike stands at the back entrance of his home, and rests his hand on the door knob. Mentally exhausted, he heaves a sigh as he looks back to Frank's truck parked in the alley behind. The cicadas quiet down, for a moment, as a stronger breeze rustles through the trees, and they resume as he opens the kitchen door.

Entering the house, Mike is seen briefly through the kitchen window before crossing to the other room. Suddenly, from inside, there is a flash of light followed simultaneously by the sound of a single gunshot. Another blast of a gunshot follows... Then, only silence.

The door at the front of the house opens and closes, and then a car engine starts up. The sheriff's patrol car shifts into gear, rolls backward out of the driveway, and pulls away from its spot behind the deputy's car. The retreating police vehicle stops in the street, shifts to a forward gear and slowly drives away.

~*~

Behind Mike's house, on the bench of the pickup truck, sit the pad of notes, police file folders and the voice recorder. Reaching into the cab of Frank's truck, a hand gathers the papers and recorder from the seat. As the late afternoon sun begins to lower behind the trees, Mary clutches the collection of files to her chest and scurries off down the alleyway.

Chapter 35

Outside of town, the Connolly trailer, with abandoned cars filling the property, is much the same as it has always been. As the afternoon daylight fades, John slinks around one of the vehicles and approaches the front door of the trailer home. Quickly, he ducks back to hide behind one of the vehicles, as approaching headlights appear in the driveway.

The lights shut off, then the engine, and John sees the driver door swing open. Mrs. Connolly steps out from the car. She slowly walks the treaded walkway to the trailer house door and plods up the wooden porch steps as if in a trance. John takes a quick breath and steps out into the dusky light. "Hello, Mrs. Connolly." From his hiding spot, John cautiously takes a step closer to the house and raises his voice louder so that she can hear him. "Mrs. Connolly... It's me, John."

With her hand lifted to turn the handle of the door, Mike's mother stares and doesn't turn to receive him. In a weak voice, she utters, "Go home, John."

John loudly whispers, "I need to find Mike."

"Go home…"

The smooth scars on John's cheek crinkle questioningly. He looks around to notice the darkening of the evening sky, the growing shadows, and the swelling chatter of cicadas. "Where does Mike live now?" John steps from the dimness. "I've been waiting for him here."

A lone tear forms and runs down her cheek, as a flood of emotions suddenly crack through and emerge on her face. "I said, go home."

John looks up at her on the porch stoop and realizes something has gone terribly wrong. "We have to get help."

Mike's mother stands immobile, as her inner anguish begins to break through. She pushes the door open to the stale alcohol smell of the trailer home, and John can make out the flickering light from the television set inside. Mrs. Connolly sniffles quietly, as she stands fixed in the doorway. "It's over… It's all over now."

Without looking back at John, she murmurs softly, "They tried to warn me about him, but it was too damn late. He's dead… My son is dead."

Standing below the porch steps, John gazes up at the despondent woman, as she stares through the dark doorway. He is at a complete loss for words until he finally utters, "What do we do now?"

Cicada

She drops her chin to her chest and slowly steps inside. Her quiet voice comes at him, and pierces through his heart. "It's finished. Just go away, John."

The drumming chatter of cicadas is deafening in his head as John watches the soul-crushed woman step forward and swing the door closed. Trembling with fear, he continues to stare at the entrance to the trailer home and asks feebly, "Where?"

~*~

It's a warm summer day in Burlingview, and the neighborhood streets are peaceful. There is the droning hum of a lawn mower in the distance, a gentle breeze rattles the leaves in the trees and a dust-devil dances along the shoulder of the pavement. On the roadside, a police car sits parked in the shade… like a patient hunter, waiting for its prey.

Seated comfortably behind the padded steering wheel, Sheriff Russling drinks from a coffee mug while he observes the rural community under his reign. Through the windshield, he scans the rustic townscape and places his cup on the dashboard next to the upright barrel of his pump shotgun. The car rocks slightly, as the sheriff adjusts himself on the seat, and the ceramic cup slides from its position on the dash. The cup spills his drink across the stack of papers on the passenger side seat and bounces to the floor. "Dammit…"

Russling scoots away from the spilled coffee, draws out his handkerchief and starts to wipe the mess on the seat. He mops the liquid from the papers before shaking them over the passenger side floorboard. Lowering his gaze, he spots the coffee mug and groans.

As the sheriff attends to the task of cleaning the spill, a solitary figure is reflected in the chrome of the police car's exterior spotlight. Slowly the person moves closer, and the distorted image appears to be carrying an old-fashioned, double-barreled shotgun. Stopped at the driver's side, the end of the long barrel pokes into the police vehicle's open window and rests on the ledge. "Hey, Russling…"

The sheriff turns to look at the business end of the antique shotgun and slowly lets his eyes travel to the exposed hammers, pulled back, in the cocked position. Face lowered to the wooden stock, the grim features of the older man stare down the barrels, while directing the firearm inside the car. Russling's expression of shock quickly fades to resignation.

The resounding blast of the shotgun explodes into the police car at point-blank range and a purplish cloud of spent-powder smoke rolls out from the passenger side windows. The acrid smell of burnt black-powder lingers in the smoky haze, and Russling's limp and blood-soaked body is pushed back against the driver's seat. His dead stare gazes toward the curved chrome of the exterior spotlight, as the reflected figure of the old man ambles away with the family's antique shotgun cradled under his arm.

A neighbor's dog barks in the distance, and a swelling chatter of cicadas fills the air.

The End.

If you enjoyed *Cicada*, read other stories by
Eric H. Heisner
www.leandogproductions.com

T. H. Elkman

Tale of a Wandering Cowboy

A Western novel by

Eric H. Heisner

www.leandogproductions.com

WEST TO BRAVO

A Western Novel   By Eric H. Heisner

WWW.LEANDOGPRODUCTIONS.COM

Wings of the Pirate

A high-flying Adventure Novel

By Eric H. Heisner

Limited time pre-order at:

www.inkshares.com

illustrations by

Al P. Bringas

www.leandogproductions.com

Eric H. Heisner is an award-winning writer, actor and filmmaker. He is the author of several novels: *West to Bravo, T. H. Elkman, Africa Tusk, Conch Republic* and *Short Western Tales: Friend of the Devil.*
He can be contacted at his website:
www.leandogproductions.com

Adeline Emmalei is a creative artist, student and animal lover. She spends her time between homes in Austin, Texas and Glendale, California.

Made in the USA
Coppell, TX
16 October 2023

22939969R00116